SCAREDY

Book 1 of the Adventures in Lusair

BY SHARON LEINO

Flint Hills Publishing

www.sharonleinoauthor.com

Cover & Character Art by Effie Gyf
www.effiegyf.etsy.com.

Cover Design by Amy Albright

ᚠFlint Hills Publishing
Topeka, Kansas
www.flinthillopublishing.com

Paperback ISBN 978-1-953583-32-1
Ebook ISBN 978-1-953583-33-8

Library of Congress Control Number 022901193

Printed in the U.S.A.

DEDICATION

To my granddaughter, Catherine Peters,
with love always.

CONTENTS

CHAPTER 1

"Eat dirt and die, stupid, weirdo, freak!"

Crushed in between the two class bullies, Rudy gasped, "Back up, I can't breathe." Sweat, running like a water faucet, flooded his green eyes and rolled off his freckled nose. Rudy grabbed the railing tight and wrapped his arms around it like a popsicle on a stick. "You're not going to push me off."

The weasel-eyed kid, Otis, grabbed Rudy's arm. "You're nothing but a chicken."

"Yeah," said Tank, who was built like a gorilla and twice the size of kids in his class. "We're not going to toss you over. All you have to do is walk over a teeny-weeny bridge." Before Rudy knew it, Tank had his other arm in a stranglehold.

Rudy shouted, "I'm not afraid! We're on a railroad trestle, not a bridge, and we are 50 feet above the river."

Jeers and laughter rang in his ears as he looked at the worn rusty rails blackened with age. Below him the creek moved quietly along in a slow rhythmic pace, but Rudy knew that it was just waiting to suck him under. *Why can't they understand? It'd be just my luck to get in the middle and a train would run me over and I'd have to jump in the water and drown. I'm not afraid. I have more sense than these bozos.*

The weasel-eyed kid put his mouth to Rudy's ear and bellowed, "Chicken crap—fraidy flap! It's not fifty feet above that little creek. We could jump down and not even break a leg."

Rudy knew it was ridiculous to be afraid, but he could feel himself shrink smaller and smaller as his insides quivered like Jell-O. *Where is Billy when I need him?*

Unexpectedly, the two lessened their grip on Rudy. Billy was coming toward them like a bull rushing a red cape. Pushing up the sleeves of his sweatshirt which was sweat-soaked from practicing Tae Kwon Do, he easily pushed the boys away from Rudy. He knew how to handle the troublemakers in their class. More than once, Billy had come to Rudy's rescue. "Back off," Billy snarled. "Come on, Rudy. Let's go."

Rudy's legs wobbled toward Billy as the bullies parted a way for him to leave. "Whew, just in time! I won't have to die today," he whispered

Billy's brown skin rippled as he flexed his muscles while motioning the bullies to back off. His arms were as thick as his wide neck, and he could throw the two of them around like rag dolls. Not as tall or big as Tank, Billy had a reputation of being able to hold his own in a fight. He never went out of his way to start one, but if it came his way, he gave as good as he got. Everyone knew that he broke a 7th grader's nose when the guy tried to use Billy as a punching bag. That made him a hero in the eyes of his 5th grade class. They walked right through the boys and headed down the dusty road as hoots and hollering followed them.

Rudy winced, feeling the insults hurled toward him. He kicked the dirt and sent a spray of sand in the air. "Why don't they understand that trestle is dangerous?"

"They're not going to leave you alone until you walk that bridge," Billy answered. "You know it's not dangerous. If it can hold a train, it can hold you."

"Yeah, well. What if my foot got stuck on the rail and I couldn't get it unstuck?" Rudy yelled.

"You know that wouldn't happen."

He knew his friend was right, but the words stuck in his throat. He kept on walking. The dusty path led to a side road that took them into town where a road sign read: *Welcome to Calumet, Michigan.*

The cool wind felt good on Rudy's sweaty face. "Why do I have to prove myself now that I'm 10 years old?"

Rudy thought about the two bullies that picked on him every single time they found him alone. Rudy was a fast runner and was able to avoid them most days. The beefy brute Tank was always thinking of new ways to scare him. He even tried to make him climb up to the top of the water tower near the old mine. That was just nuts! The ladder rungs went up a hundred feet high and looked old and rusted. Good thing that inspector came in the nick of time and chased them all away. Rudy outran **all** of the bullies. His mind was running wild with all the things they tried to make him do. He would never forget the time they wanted him to walk through the long, dark, wet culvert in which he couldn't even stand up. The scariest time was when he had to jump off a ledge into the lake. Thank goodness he could swim. That ledge must have been a thousand feet high—even though Billy told him it wasn't that high and people jumped off it every day. It just went on and on like this. Luckily, he had been able to talk himself out of a few situations, but lately it had become more important for him to run faster than the bullies.

The other day he was running and heard the track coach yell, "Stop! I've never seen anyone run that fast. Why don't you come by when we're training and join in. If you keep that up, I'll put you on the track team next year."

If I live long enough.

Finally, his thoughts settled, and he said to Billy, "You know that bridge **is** dangerous."

Rolling his dark eyes, Billy said, "It's not dangerous. The railroad keeps repairing it all the time. If a train can go on it, so can you."

Throwing his hands in the air, Rudy said, "Well, that creek has an undertow that will suck you under."

"Rudy, where do you get those crazy ideas? You can walk across that creek. It only comes up to your knees!"

Rudy kept quiet, but his thoughts ran on. *I need to stop watching scary movies. Maybe my imagination does run away with me. Life sure can just be difficult at times. I just have to be prepared for the worst. That doesn't mean I'm afraid!*

Rudy walked across the rolling green lawn until he came to a large oak tree. His eyes moved up, up, up to the top. There sat his new tree house just waiting for him to make the climb. His father insisted the tree house be built up high, but did it have to be built in the clouds?

He could hear his father saying, "It's not a hundred feet high, it's a foot taller than me. No, I'm not a giant. Besides, you have to take a chance and try new things. It's perfectly safe."

Safe. Dad had a funny idea of what safe was. He was always testing the limits of everything. *Who ever heard of an old guy who was 50 going skydiving? He must have a death wish. And what about the time he and Mom went parasailing in Mexico? How crazy was that! Didn't they watch Jurassic Park with me?* He slumped down against the tree, exhausted from trying to make sense of it all.

Billy interrupted his thoughts. "Let's go fishing."

"After lunch," Rudy mumbled.

"Then, let's go up. . . "

"Don't feel like it," Rudy said.

Billy flopped down next to Rudy. "Why are you always scared? Just try it. It's not going to kill ya."

"You sound just like my dad. I'm not afraid," he said, pulling his knees up and hugging them.

"If you'd just try. . . "

Rudy thumped his head against the tree. "I don't want to."

"How can someone so smart with books be such a dork and make up things to be afraid of?"

Rudy's face turned an angry red as he got in Billy's face and looked into his black eyes. They stared at each other for a long time without saying a word. Rudy got dizzy.

Jumping up and climbing to the tree house, Billy called, "Come on!"

A challenge. "Just a minute." He knew he had to try. The only problem was that anything higher than two pairs of socks made his stomach queasy. Halfway up, his foot slipped. Panicking, Rudy let go and landed spread-eagle on his back. His frizzy hair spread out like hundreds of dried red worms.

Billy covered his mouth so he wouldn't laugh. "That was only a little fall. Try again."

Rudy couldn't talk. It felt like an elephant was sitting on his chest, whooshing all the air out of him. Staggering to his feet, clutching his chest, he heard his mother call him for lunch. All he could do was wave goodbye.

Walking into the kitchen, he felt air coming back into his lungs. His mother turned and asked, "Were you and Billy up in the tree house?"

"Naw, Billy and I are going fishing."

"Just remember, if you bring home a whale, you are the one that will have to boil the blubber."

Rudy stared at his mother. "Are you kidding?" Laughing, she placed his sandwich on the table and told him he was way too serious.

Ten minutes later, Billy yelled through the screen door, "Are you finished yet?"

"Come in, Billy." He walked in with a fishing pole in one hand and a half-eaten sandwich in the other.

Stuffing the rest of the sandwich in his mouth, Rudy ran to his room to get his fishing gear. He emerged with a fishing pole and a **huge** backpack. He leaned forward with his hands on his knees and adjusted the pack.

Billy groaned. "What the heck? Where do you think we're going? On an African safari? What's in that?"

He took the backpack off and sat it on the floor. "First, we have snacks. Then a tent, hooks, sinkers, extra line, bug spray, Band-Aids, silver ribbon. . . "

Billy glared at Rudy. "You don't need all that stuff. We're only going for an hour. And what's with that huge roll of silver ribbon?"

"The last time we went fishing you said I needed something shiny on my hook to attract the fish. Wa-Lah! The silver ribbon! Besides, you never know when this other stuff will come in handy. And you don't have to carry it."

7

"The only thing you need is snacks. It's a wonder you didn't bring a compass in case we got lost. Like we've only been to this lake a hundred times," Billy muttered, as he headed for the door.

Rudy let the door slam, "I did bring a compass! You never know when you're going to get lost."

They walked out the back door to the wooden gate in the fence. Once they got through, Rudy made sure it was latched. Walking on the gravel road, the stones crunched under their feet. It was the only sound heard for a long time.

Rudy knew Billy was staring at him and couldn't take it anymore. "What?"

"Look at you. You're going to topple over with that backpack."

"Oh yeah? It's easy to be brave when you've got arms like a tree and can beat up a 7th grader. Besides, I'm not afraid. I may be puny, but I'm only being prepared and not taking chances."

More silence. They came to a forest with trees that grew taller with the rising hill. Leaves rustled in the warm breeze. The sun sent shafts of rays into the shaded forest as birds flited from tree to tree singing songs of welcome.

Billy pointed. "I know a shortcut through those trees."

"We could get lost."

"Argh! We won't get lost. Nothing will get us. No evil wizards, or knights, or boogie men are in there!" Billy marched up the hill with his fishing pole on his shoulder. "You can come with me if you want or stay there."

Sagging under the weight of his backpack, Rudy slowly followed Billy, each slow step feeling heavy. They entered the woods as trees stretched forever upward. It was dark and shadowy except for small rays of sun penetrating through clusters of leaves.

"Isn't this cool? It's like going into another world! Wouldn't it be neat if we did meet a wizard or knights in their armor?" Bowing grandly, with black dreadlocks falling and covering his face, Billy said, "Sir knight, I am here to serve the king."

Rudy's eyes darted back and like a chameleon, watching and waiting for something to happen. "Quit clowning around. Let's hurry and get out of here. It's weird."

Billy laughed. "Weird? This is great! Look at the way the leaves arch overhead. It looks like we're about to enter a different world!"

Rudy leaned with his hands on his knees to balance the backpack. "Do it by yourself. I just want to get out of here." He noticed large sun rays streaming through an opening in the trees. "Whew. We're almost there."

Billy darted ahead and the sun rays exploded into a blinding light.

Rudy closed his eyes, and when he opened them, he couldn't believe what he saw. A large man, covered in armor and boots made of bronze, gleamed in the sunlight. He sat on a huge white horse that took a step forward. He was so close that when the horse blew air out of its nostrils, it made Rudy's hair flutter up. The gold on his belt caught a ray of sun that split the light and surrounded him and his horse. He took off his helmet revealing eyes that looked like flames of fire. Snow white hair fell to his shoulders. Slowly, he took off one of his metal gauntlets and extended his hand toward Rudy. In his hand was a key—as big as a football—on a silver chain that had no beginning and no end. The ground shook when his thunderous voice said, "Fear must be faced and overcome. If not, it leads to destruction—hate—chaos. You are needed in the north."

Rudy felt his red hair standup, "That thing must weigh a ton! How am I supposed to wear it? Which way is north? Where am I even at?"

The knight's thunderous voice continued, "Take this key and wear it. Enter through Kneelgrove. Use the key for your journey. No one can take it from you. It will keep you safe."

Rudy tried to step to the side of the great horse when he stumbled and slid face first through the circle of light, while at the same time watching the Knight of Light place the chain over his head. He looked at the key around his neck. It was the size of a regular door key. *How did he make it smaller? It's as light as a feather.*

Sitting up and looking around, he discovered the lake was gone. Everything that should have been there was gone. The creaky dock, the spooky sunken boat—gone. No one was fishing. There were always other people fishing on the lake—no one was anywhere. *What am I going to do?*

10

In its place, there was a tired, worn meadow yellowed with spots of dirt. Small tiny flowers, weak and pale in color, waved slowly in the sparse grass. Tall pines stood on each side, as though guarding it from an imminent death. The chirring of the crickets was the only noise he heard. *Noisy little buggers.*

He couldn't take it anymore. Throwing off his backpack and running, first to the left and then to the right, he shouted, "Billy! Billy! Where are you? This isn't funny. Someone stole the lake."

He stopped and listened. Nothing, absolutely nothing. Even the crickets were quiet. He called for Billy over and over. Angry, he looked toward the woods. "This isn't funny, Billy. Where are you hiding?" No one answered. The woods suddenly looked dark and scary. Somehow, it looked **alive**. Small shadows were moving and running, making weird sharp hooting and whistling noises.

"That's not funny Billy. You're just trying to scare me. Well, it won't work!" Rudy shouted. Turning to grab his backpack, he saw the pack running down the hill, eight tiny feet emerging from the bottom!

CHAPTER 2

"ARGGGGGG!" *What's going on?* Rudy couldn't believe his eyes. Running, he caught up with the backpack and yanked it into the air. Underneath the pack, hanging on with all their might, were four creatures no bigger than a piglet barely a foot tall. They even looked like piglets except they had hands and feet and were covered in fur. They wore pants, but no shoes. And talk about being dirty! Rudy just stared at them.

Finally, one spoke, "My name is Purloin and we are Furlets of the Land." They all let go and dropped to the ground in front of Rudy.

Rudy sat down on the backpack to make sure they didn't take it again and then looked at the piglets smeared with dirt and fur badly in need of brushing. "Why did you take my backpack?"

The furlets looked at each other and shrugged their shoulders. Purloin looked at Rudy and said, "We always take things. That is what we do."

"Just like that, you take things? What kind of excuse is that for stealing?"

Purloin and the other furlets puffed up their tiny chests and put their hands on their hips and bellowed together, "We don't steal, we borrow!"

Rudy couldn't believe how powerful and loud the voices were coming from such tiny creatures. He decided to change the subject, "I've lost my friend Billy. Have you seen another boy here with blue shorts and a red shirt?"

The furlets looked surprised at Rudy's question, and then began laughing so hard they fell down, rolling around on the ground. Their laughter was so contagious that Rudy had to cover his mouth so he wouldn't join in.

"Doesn't your friend Billy wear pants? What is he doing running around in his shorts?" Purloin couldn't continue because he had another fit of laughter.

Now that Rudy knew what they were laughing at, he was losing patience. "He is wearing shorts like mine. Only mine are brown and his are blue."

Puzzled, Purloin looked at Rudy. "I thought those were pants that you outgrew. Shorts are underwear around here." The furlets laughed again, rolling around on the ground when suddenly they scattered and disappeared.

Rudy felt a great weight land on his back. A voice whispered, "Move and you're a dead man."

Rudy froze. He believed the voice and did not twitch an eyelash. Suddenly, he heard laughter as he was rolled over on top of his backpack.

Rudy felt his body flush with heat from rage. Struggling to get Billy off his back, he pushed Billy down and jumped on him. "You rotten. . . "

Billy easily fended off Rudy's attack. Rudy jumped up and tried again. Billy circled Rudy and grabbed him in a lock hold. "Calm down! What are you so mad about?" When Rudy stopped thrashing around and became still, Billy let him go.

Rudy tried to attack Billy again. This time Billy flipped him on the ground and sat on him. Rudy howled and yelled all sorts of things.

"My, my, where did you learn such language?"

Exhausted, he whimpered, "Why did you hide from me?"

Billy got off Rudy and helped him up. "Hmm, were you scared?"

"ABSOLUTELY NOT! I was confused and lost and worried about where you were." In quieter tones, he added, "I thought you were my friend."

Billy put his hand on Rudy's shoulder. "I was lost. I know this sounds crazy, but I went back into the woods and went through that circle of light behind you, but then I couldn't find you. I finally saw you on the hill. By the time I got there, you were gone. I tried to call, but you were hollering so much I don't think you heard me. When I got to the top of the hill, I saw a castle. Didn't you see the castle? What a battle. . . "

"Castle? Battle?" Rudy finally stood up and looked around. He couldn't believe his eyes. On the next hill was a smoldering castle. Its walls were charred and blackened from fire. The moat that surrounded the castle was full of gray steaming water. Its battered drawbridge hung lopsided, half raised. Flags were torn and strewn all over the ground.

"Wow! How did I miss that? Must've been some battle." Rudy whispered. "The walls are still smoking. I wonder what happened?"

Below the castle, the streets were lined with small houses that had straw roofs. The roofs were blackened with gaping holes, smoking like the castle walls. Cooking fires burned in the center of the village with children huddled around them. Fences were destroyed, and animals and people milled aimlessly about as though looking for something or someone.

Rudy shielded his eyes and looked to the right of the castle. He saw a gloomy swamp surrounded by black water that rippled with white objects. He rubbed his eyes. "Are those bones?" Stumbling, he landed on his backpack and sat for several moments. "I'm in another world! We don't have castles in Michigan!"

Billy stared at Rudy and couldn't figure out why he was acting like he hadn't seen any of this before. "When you were sitting on the backpack, didn't you see the castle and the destruction?"

"Huh, no, I was talking to furlets." Rudy turned and grabbed his backpack.

Billy looked at Rudy. "Furlets? What are you talking about? Let's go check out that castle and maybe we'll see a dragon along the way." Billy was so excited that he jumped up and ran, thrusting his arm about as though he had a sword. He wasn't listening as Rudy tried to explain what furlets were. Excited, he talked on and on about knights and dragons.

Rudy scanned the sky. "Dragons? Billy, do you really think there are dragons here?"

"I don't know, but it sure would be neat to see them flying around and belching fire."

"Are you crazy?! Belching fire and frying us to a crisp! What are you thinking?"

Billy stopped and looked at Rudy. "Now that is the first sensible thing you have said in a long time. I guess I don't really want to see one, but it would be neat to ride on one."

Rudy stared at the castle. "I don't think we are going to get there before it gets dark. It must be miles away. Bet you're glad I brought the tent now."

Billy laughed and clapped him on the back. "Let's get moving and see how far we get."

They walked in silence. Rudy felt bad that he had dampened Billy's excitement. *I guess it would be fun to see a dragon, IF he wouldn't burn us to smithereens.* But there was another, more pressing thought weighing on Rudy's mind. "Billy, how are we going to get home?"

"Home? We just got here. We need to go to the castle and

see what happened. Come on!" Billy laughed, and the tension seemed to ease, although they were both quiet for a long time each with their own thoughts.

The sky was beautiful, but Rudy noticed certain trees were suffering. Their towering branches were broken from a slimy rot that oozed out from the bark of the tree. "What kind of disease do you think these trees have?"

"You're the genius. What am I? A tree-ologist? Look at that giant pine tree. Its branches are sweeping the ground. That thing must be 100 feet tall, but it doesn't look healthy!"

"It's called a Norway Weeping spruce. Don't you remember the field trip we took to the park and the guide told us that it would grow anywhere from 50 to 80 feet? It sure is a paler green than the one we saw in the park and has a lot fewer of those long skinny pinecones."

The sun was starting to set when they arrived at another Norway Weeping spruce that looked healthier than the others. Billy pulled several pine branches back and walked under the boughs. "Wow, this is so cool. I can stand up in here. Come on in. This is like a fort. Can you see me? I'm sure you can't. What a neat hiding place." Billy pushed back the boughs and urged Rudy to come inside. "These branches are thick. Nothing will see us."

"What if there's an animal in there?" Rudy hesitated. "I'm not afraid, I'm just thinking of all the possibilities. We can't be too careful."

Billy rolled his eyes. "I was inside. I walked all the way around the tree. Did you hear me yell that there was an animal? NO. Think about what you're saying. And STOP thinking about all the possibilities. Would I be this calm if there was an animal in here?"

Rudy held his breath and passed by Billy, who pushed him ahead. Nothing moved or made a sound under the tree, and they were swept inside as Billy let go of the branches.

Rudy landed on a blanket of long brown pine needles. "Wow, this is like a fort! There are so many pine needles here that when I fell it was like falling on a soft carpet. Why couldn't my dad just let me build something like this?"

"Think, Rudy. You don't have giant pines like this in your yard." Billy stood near the trunk and looked up as the last light of the day poked through the small fingers of the boughs. "Guess we'll be safe here. I'm sure no one can find us. Why don't you get that flashlight out before it gets really dark?"

Rudy pulled out the FlashTorch, the brightest of all flashlights. Though the sun had set and darkness had settled in, underneath the tree it was bright as day. Rudy had no trouble pulling out the sleeping bags and arranging their sleeping area. He was exhausted and too tired to be afraid of the night. "This is a safe place. No one will find us here." No sooner had the words left his mouth than they heard a noise outside the branches.

"Agg!" He felt something hit the bottom of his feet and saw a pile of dirt. Jumping up they saw a huge mound of dirt with hands and feet sticking out of it. All at once, it began shaking like a dog that just got out of a lake. It shook dirt in all directions, quickly covering Billy and Rudy. When the dirt storm stopped, they wiped their eyes and saw a tall, thin form standing before them. A bald man with large round eyes capped with scraggly eyebrows brushed the dirt from his large, pointed ears. His head tilted back and forth as he examined the two boys. He waved his arms and all the dirt disappeared from him, Rudy, and Billy.

"Awesome," said Billy, as he watched the dirt roll away and sink back into the ground.

Wearing a long leather coat that covered everything except the tips of his boots Rudy thought the man looked like a scarecrow. His square squat hat was crooked, showing patches of white curls on a balding head.

Billy asked, "What and who are you? How did you tunnel under the tree and pop out of the ground?"

"I am called Nipron. Now, who are you?"

"I'm Billy and the one with his mouth hanging open is Rudy. What are you?"

Nipron frowned, not sure what to make of the two boys. "I'm a questor, which means caretaker of the Earth. What are you doing here?"

Rudy brushed off the remaining dirt. "We're lost. We started to go fishing and found a castle."

"How can you go fishing and get lost?"

"We came out of the woods and ended up in a different world," Billy said.

"Hmm, you could be from a different world. We occasionally have people from other worlds come here. And you are dressed in outlandish outfits. Why are your pants cut off at your knees? And your shirt sleeves—did they shrink? And look at these shoes, very colorful, but what is that material that they are made of? How did you get here?"

When Nipron finally stopped asking questions, Billy explained that they were wearing T-shirts and shorts and that their gym shoes were made from rubber. Nipron still looked skeptical but remained quiet.

Rudy murmured. "I met a knight on a horse. He was so full of light and his eyes were on fire. Even so, he made me feel safe."

"You saw a knight? I didn't see a knight. All I saw was a great circle of light that I walked through," Billy said.

"The Knight of Light?" Nipron's eyes were large and his voice sharp. "How can that be? He never comes in contact with humans."

Not wanting to upset Nipron anymore, Rudy quietly said, "He gave me a key and said we are needed in the north and that it would protect us."

Nipron staggered, clutching his chest. "Are you telling the truth? Let me see this so-called key."

Rudy pulled it out from under his T-shirt.

"That looks like my father's key that he used to wear." He was quiet for a long time. "Maybe the Knight of Light sent you to help. We are at war with evil. A wicked wizard wants to rule the world."

Nipron began to describe how everything was turning black with disease and decay. Crops failed and people were hungry. Lightning would strike homes on a sunny day without warning, destroying everything. "More than that," he lowered his voice to a whisper, "neighbors used to be friends but that has all changed They are fearful. And the fear has turned to hate. Happiness and their peaceful way of life is lost. No matter what anyone has tried, this disease of fear, hate, and distrust has spread like a plague. We must go back to the forest to see if we can find the knight."

Rudy couldn't believe it. "What? Are you nuts?!"

CHAPTER 3

"Wow!" Billy exclaimed. "An evil wizard?"

Rudy closed his eyes. "Why did I have to end up here? We're just kids, we can't help you. Can't you get rid of one wizard? We don't even know what your world is all about and we certainly have no power!" he shouted. He stopped and tried to remember everything he'd learned about knights and castles in school. "But if you have a castle, you must have lots of knights. "Can't the knights get rid of this wizard?"

"No! They are under his evil spell." Nipron's scraggly eyebrows trembled. "He has turned their thinking around. They think that everything evil is good and everything good is evil. They don't know what they are doing."

"If the knights can't help, then how can we?" Rudy put his head in his hands. "This can't be happening."

"Rudy, this is a chance of a lifetime! What do you mean we can't help? The knight told you the key would protect you," Billy replied.

Rudy kept shaking his head, "This can't be happening. It

can't be real."

"Not real? Now listen here, young man. We do have knights!"

"Okay, okay!" Rudy held up his hands in surrender. "I still don't know how we can help. . . " The rest of his words drifted away as thoughts tumbled into his mind. *Maybe we can get lost again and find our way home.* "On second thought, why don't we go back to the forest? Maybe we can find some answers there. That's where I met your Knight of Light."

Glaring at him suspiciously, Nipron wondered why Rudy had changed his mind so quickly. But he was tired from the day's events and yawned, "My brain is too tired to think. Tomorrow morning will be soon enough. It has been a trying day and I need to get some rest."

Rudy thought, *He had a trying day? What about me? Try ending up in a different world where there is an evil wizard!* But he was so tired he just settled into the sleeping bag and turned off the flashlight. Nipron had taken a small ball of light out of his pocket and hung it on a branch above, adding warmth. Rudy wiggled into the soft needles until he found a comfortable position. In the darkness, he could hear the slow breathing of Nipron. Rudy whispered to Billy, "The forest must be the way to go back home. It's got to be the way home." But Billy fell asleep before Rudy finished talking.

CRCRCR

Rudy woke to find Nipron and Billy gone. He scrambled out from under the branches. It was too quiet. So still, no wind blowing. Then he saw them, standing like frozen statues. He rushed over to see if they were still breathing. They were! "What are you guys doing?"

They didn't answer. Nor did they move a muscle or bat an eyelash. He touched them—they were rigid but alive. He heard a rustling noise behind him. Standing perfectly still, Rudy saw movement from the corner of his eye. A wrinkled, squatty man hobbled slowly toward them. A bright purple feather in his crumpled hat bobbed to and fro with each step he took. High in the air, he held a small silver hammer that quivered in the sunlight. Turning, Rudy accidentally tripped and fell on the tiny man. The hammer went flying. At the same time, Nipron and Billy were able to move.

Catching the hammer, Nipron hung on to it. "How dare you! How many times have I warned you about that hammer, Dinky?"

Dinky pushed Rudy off and said, "I know how to use the hammer. Besides, it was the only way I could get you to stand still so I could talk to you. You're always on the run. You know I'm supposed to be with you. Who else would take care of you?"

"I thought I ridded myself of you back at the palace," Nipron snapped.

Dinky stretched to his full height, all three feet of him. "Why would you want to be rid of me?" He stomped his foot. "Diddly squat! I'm the one that helped you escape."

Billy stared at Dinky, unable to curb his curiosity. He had never seen a person with so many wrinkles. "Aha, you're a dwarf, aren't you?"

Standing in front of Billy with his hands on his hips, he snarled, "Yeah, wanna make something of it?"

"No, no, I didn't mean anything by it! This is such a new world. I get excited and just blurt things out."

Dinky laughed, "Aww, that's okay. Just had to be sure you weren't making fun. Not nice, you know."

Rudy ran his hand through his red hair. "How did the hammer freeze them into statues?"

Dinky was proud of his silver hammer as it was a legend among the dwarfs and part of his heritage. "Eons ago, we used to carve cities beneath the earth. They were great cities of beauty and light. We found sources of light-rocks that light up the darkness underground. But the Demon of Chaos tried to destroy us by sending his serfs to spread evil. The Knight of Light gave us these hammers to freeze them into statues to stop the spread of evil in our clans. The evil serfs would spend the rest of their days frozen as statues."

Nipron's voice was low and slow like a bull pawing at the dirt waiting to charge. "Dinky, you know you are supposed to use that under the earth." Spitting out each word he said, "Not. On. Top. Of. The. Earth!"

Before he could respond, Rudy interrupted. He didn't want to listen to a lengthy argument. "Don't you think we should be on our way to find the Knight of Light?"

"Knight of Light? Diddly! Have you lost your mind? We are

not supposed to find the Knight of Light. He is supposed to come to us!"

"Why? He gave me a special key and said we need to head north."

Dinky ran over and looked at the key Rudy was wearing. He couldn't figure out why the key was given to someone from a different world, and a human to boot.

Rudy said again, "Shouldn't we be on our way? It's going to take all day to go back to the forest."

Billy looked at the castle and the people wandering aimlessly. "Shouldn't we see if we can help those people?"

Nipron shook his head no. "I was there before I met you. I did as much as I could. It is now up to them. They need to learn to heal together. To work and regain the trust they once had. Only they can do that. We should not interfere. We have more urgent matters and need to head north to find the Knight of Light. We have wasted enough time."

Nipron took a new path that was difficult to walk because the grass was long and seemed to have a life of its own! It grabbed and wrapped around Rudy and Billy's legs, refusing to let go.

Scowling, Rudy pulled his legs up, one after the other in a marching rhythm, tearing the grass from its grasp as he walked.

Billy said, "We are never going to make it to the forest before dark with this grass trying to hold us in one place."

Dinky and Nipron were having an easy time walking through the grass. It left them completely alone.

"Diddly squat! All you have to do is think about a goat eating the grass and it will stay away."

Rudy was frustrated enough that he decided to try it and envisioned six goats eating the grass. Immediately, the grass parted and lay flat on the ground. *Thank goodness!* He needed to save all his energy to carry that heavy backpack. He couldn't help but walk like an old man with his nose close to the ground.

Billy felt sorry for Rudy and offered to take turns carrying the backpack. The air was fresh and clean. The clouds high above were beautiful and kept changing shapes. He watched one cloud turn into a dragon that twirled and whirled in flight. He was too tired to speak but was determined to lift his head so that he could watch the beautiful sight. After hours of walking, stands of trees came into view. "Shade," he murmured.

They stopped under the coolness of the trees and collapsed on the ground, wiping the sweat that dripped from their faces. "Good thing I brought water. You know, Billy. You need to thank me for bringing this stuff along."

"I thought I was saying thanks by helping you carry that backpack part of the way," Billy grumbled.

After resting, they continued to walk and came to the top of a waterfall. Bending over, they watched the water gush as it cascaded down the canyon, roaring as it hit the bottom. Suddenly, an ear-piercing noise filled their ears. They heard the sound again. This time closer, as though it was moving upward from the bottom of the waterfall. A pointed head with jaws wide open appeared at the edge of the cliff and they found themselves staring in the blue eyes of a dragon! His eyeballs rotated like prisms that were trying to pull their thoughts into his. The dragon's skin was not wrinkled or leathery but had white silken scales running up and down its body. It shined as it perched on the edge of the cliff. A flap of its wings sent everyone tumbling backwards. Though large and fearsome, it soon became clear there was no threat. The creature spoke into each of their minds with a deep rolling sound, *Nipron, what are you doing here?* He stood regally with wings spread, iridescent colors shining and rotating all around him.

"Sagacious! What a relief. I have looked everywhere for you. We need your help. Evil is taking over our world."

Nipron, the dragon responded telepathically, *I know the world is dying from this evil. But I need to remind you that I cannot interfere in your world.*

"But this is different. The rules do not apply anymore. All the questors and healers have been killed. I am the only one left. And even then, I do not have all the knowledge that is needed."

A deep rumbling, vibrating noise emerged from the dragon's throat. The news troubled him deeply. *So cruel, so sad. Nipron, you know I would help if I could. But even though there is evil and chaos, you know the rules still apply."*

Holding back tears, Nipron squinted one eye as he looked at

Sagacious, his voice heavy with sorrow, "I know you are right. It was just a slip of my thoughts. Of course our rules must apply or we would have anarchy, which is almost what we have now."

Sagacious eyes rotated even faster. *You need to believe in yourself and know you can take care of this. The Knight of Light has sent you the key. The only thing I can tell you is to head north.*

"You, too? The Knight of Light talks to everyone but me!" Defeated, Nipron hunched his shoulders and put his head down as he walked away. He had nothing else to say. He knew that he couldn't ask Sagacious for help, but he was desperate. For the first time in his life, he did not know what to do. Dinky and Rudy followed.

Billy was so fascinated by Sagacious he could not move an inch. Finally, he was able to ask in a husky voice, "I saw a cloud in the sky that turned into a dragon and flew away. Was that you?"

Laughter rumbled in Sagacious' chest. *Yes, very few humans are able to see what you saw. You have a special sight for a human. Take care, Billy. Your courage is strong, and you will need it for your journey."*

Sagacious sprang into the air, his wings sounding like rushing wind. At one point, he started to scatter into pieces, and then came together to form a cloud of dark blue. With a wink of an eye, he disappeared.

Billy finally caught up with the others as they headed for the forest that had brought them into this funny world. He couldn't help but smile at having the honor of meeting Sagacious. Rudy, on the other hand, wiped the sweat from his brow and was glad that the huge dragon was gone. They walked for hours in silence, listening to crickets chirping and the occasional bird that flew overhead. Nipron was deep in thought and not watching where he was going.

"It's a good thing I am walking beside you," said Dinky.

Nipron looked up just as Dinky stopped him and pulled him back. The next step would have plunged Nipron off a cliff that was high above the forest.

"It is taking a lot longer to get to the woods. Are you sure you know how to get back to the forest?" Rudy asked. "We didn't come this way because I never saw a waterfall, a dragon, or a cliff with the forest below it."

Nipron shook his head. "Well, there is the forest. Sorry, I was so deep in thought I must have taken a wrong turn. We will be there before you know it."

They turned to go down the path when lightning landed at Rudy's feet. "Argh!" Yelling and jumping backwards, he bumped into Dinky, tripped, and landed on top of him. Scrambling up, he saw a Dark Knight charging toward him on a horse that had savage eyes and was snorting smoke. Rudy panicked, turned, and without looking where he was going, he ran and fell over the cliff. Billy grabbed Dinky and quickly backed away from the ledge. The jewel at the end of Nipron's staff flashed streaks of glowing light, causing the Dark Knight to break into millions of pieces.

"Billy, Dinky, get back here. Where is Rudy?" Nipron asked.

Billy and Dinky walked to where Nipron was standing. They looked all around for Rudy and couldn't see him but heard a faint call for help. They ran over to the edge of the cliff and saw Rudy hanging. His backpack had caught on a sharp point of a boulder.

"Help! I don't want to die!" Right then, one of the straps slipped. Just as quickly, Nipron reached his staff out and pulled Rudy and his backpack up. Rudy landed face down and stayed there for a few minutes.

"Rudy, you're safe now. You can get up," Billy said as he tugged on the backpack. "Let me help you."

"NO! I am never getting up."

While hiding his staff once again inside his cloak, Nipron quietly asked, "Are you going to lay there and wait for another Dark Knight to come?"

Wild-eyed, Rudy jumped up and said, "Let's go."

Turning around and following a worn path down the cliff, they trudged along. The sun was fading in the sunset when the forest came into view. The woods were pitch black.

"Uh, don't you think we should wait until morning to go into the woods? Can't you hear those weird noises?" Rudy asked.

"I can see in the dark, so we might as well keep going," replied Nipron.

"Diddly, Nipron—you might not need a light, but we do. If we can't see, we may end up walking into a tree or something worse," said Dinky.

Just then, a huge bat swooped out of the woods toward the small group. Its wings were six feet wide. Billy and Rudy hit the dirt yelling. Nipron and Dinky just stared at them not understanding their fear. "That's just a fruit bat! Diddly squat! He won't hurt you."

Standing up, Billy wiped the dirt from his face. "I've never seen a bat that big! I don't care if he is just a fruity bat. I'm not going into the woods tonight."

Still lying on the ground with his arms over his head Rudy muttered, "I'm with Billy. I'm not going into the woods either."

CHAPTER 4

"If we must, we must." Nipron took a ball of light out of his pocket. It was a small, low light that only lit his face.

Rudy said, "We need a brighter light."

"Hold on, Rudy. Let me get your gigantic trucker, Flash Torch." Billy reached into the backpack and found the flashlight. He turned it on, lighting up the area surrounding them.

Dinky, fearful of the light, ran and crashed into Nipron, knocking him down. "Argg! Ratch's workers!" he exclaimed.

"What's the matter?" Billy asked.

"You diddling dwarf! Get off me," Nipron said as he struggled to get up. "They're boys from another world, not wizards."

"It's still magic!" Dinky stomped his foot. "Don't you remember what Ratch did at the palace?"

"Who's Ratch?" Rudy asked.

"An evil man. . . " Dinky couldn't stop shaking his finger at them or yelling. His words came out fast and clipped. "Wizard! One who's immersed in black magic who sold his soul to the Demon of Chaos. He uses serfs from the underworld that are not alive. These serfs torture those who don't agree with Ratch and rip out their guts."

"Be quiet!" Nipron's penetrating glare froze Dinky's lips tightly shut. "Ratch is the name of the evil wizard I told you about. He is evil, and has sold his soul to the underworld, but we must stop him. The only way to stop him is to find the Knight of Light."

"But you didn't say he sold his soul to the Demon of Chaos! Or that his serfs torture and rip out guts!" interrupted Billy.

Sighing deeply, Nipron shrugged his shoulders, "I never said it was going to be easy. But there are ways that we can protect you . . ."

Dinky interrupted, "Yeah, Nipron can do a lot of things that will keep us out of reach of the wizard."

Once again, Nipron glared at Dinky who was suddenly quiet. "If we work together, we can get this job done. We will do what the Knight of Light tells us to do. I'm sure there will be more instructions as we go along. Now, turn off that light. We don't want to alert things of the night that we are here. Let's settle in next to that umbrella tree."

Rudy mumbled, "Things of the night? Umbrella tree?"

Darkness was creeping around them. They moved quietly and stopped at the gnarled tree whose trunk bent to the right and then jutted straight up in the air. Its large, low branches spread out like an umbrella with small bits of foliage scattered on top.

Taking the plastic tent and pegs out of his backpack, Rudy said, "We can throw the tent over the branches."

Just as he and Billy finished pounding the pegs into the ground, Dinky rushed inside. Rudy stared at the forest until a vicious howl broke the quiet, sending him quickly into the tent.

Billy, sitting next to Dinky, said, "Boy, am I hungry."

"I've got just the thing." Dinky opened a small brown bag and pulled out food. A large, round wheel of cheese appeared, a long loaf of bread, peach pie, and a flask. Eager hands grabbed for the food.

Between bites, Rudy asked, "How did all that stuff come out of that little bag?"

"It's magic. I stole it from Ratch." Dinky took a large bite of pie. "I used to watch him from the terrace in the castle. He wouldn't eat any of the food from the banquet table that he had his workers fix. He only ate from this bag."

Food sprayed from Rudy and Billys' mouths. "Is this food **evil**?" asked Rudy.

Nipron reached for the cheese. "Of course not! Ratch has to eat food just like the rest of us. He just would not eat from the banquet table because he put spells on the food. He did that to control the people, just one method he used. He has even more ways to torture families, threatening them with death."

Billy and Rudys' eyes watered as they choked down this food, wondering if it was okay to eat.

"Just what has this Ratch done?" Rudy asked.

Lowering their heads, Dinky and Nipron were quiet for a long time. In a low voice, and choking back tears, Nipron began to tell the story of what had happened at the castle. "The people who lived there were healers and teachers. Everyone across the land loved them because they would heal anyone who came to them, and they charged nothing. They taught people better ways to live, to eat healthy, the best way to raise crops, and how to raise the best livestock. The most important thing they taught was how to be kind to one another and how to treat others with love and respect."

Wide eyed, Rudy asked in a shaky voice, "What happened to the healers?"

Tears flooded Niporon's eyes and ran down his cheeks. He coughed, and in a raspy voice said, "At night, Ratch called the Demons of Chaos to destroy the village and to burn the castle. There was a fierce battle at the castle. Lightning came from the sky and up from the ground, lighting fires everywhere. While the wind whipped the fires into a frenzy, flames swirled high, acting as though they had fingers touching everything in sight. The fire seemed to have a life of its own as it danced and swirled and stretched until everything was on fire. People tried to get away but couldn't. An invisible wall held them there." Nipron's voice broke into sobs. It was a while before he could continue. "The people you saw wandering the village were seeking the healers." Nipron's globe flared while he was talking. "They watched the horror. Lightning flashes created fires on the roof tops, in the streets, in the water, and in the fields. Fiery debris and ash, smoke and flames, swirled around everything, destroying it all. People were running, trying to escape, with nowhere to go. The fires were burning everything and everyone. The cries of the people still ring in my ears. They tried to run out of their village, but an invisible wall held them there. Smoke rose high into the air as flames licked the sky. Soon the smoke poured out of the globe and dimmed the light."

Rudy could almost smell the smoke and feel the pain of the people. He hid his face and wiped the tears away. "How could that happen?"

Billy scrubbed his face from the tears on his cheeks and in a soft voice asked, "How could fire spread so quickly? I don't understand why you couldn't stop it?"

"Ratch threw up a shield that acted like a wall around the castle and everything near it. It blocked anyone from going into the village and anyone from leaving. Ratch quenched the fires with black sewer-like water full of decay and disease. The water stank worse than rotten eggs. There was so much of the black water that it ran into the lake next to the castle and a swamp was the result." Nipron paused and scrubbed his face with his hands. In a tired and defeated voice he said, "I really don't know why I couldn't break through that wall to rescue them."

Rudy could hardly speak but asked, "Why did Ratch do that?"

Harsh brittle tones filled the tent. "To break the spirit of the people. To make sure they would do anything he wanted them to do. To keep them hostage. Hostages, so that they would not depend on the healers, but to depend on him. To be at his command at will!"

Rudy paled and wondered if he'd ever see home again.

"How can the Knight of Light stop Ratch?" Billy asked.

Dinky stood up, stomped his foot, and pounded his fist. "Diddly squat! We have no business trying to find the Knight of Light. Did you know that a person could die or disappear just by looking at him? He is powerful and punishes those who call him for no reason. Besides, he has to be invited to our world."

Die? Disappear? Maybe I'm not alive. What a choice. A wizard that burns everyone up or a knight that makes you disappear when you don't agree with him. Rudy felt sick to his stomach.

"Silly fool." Nipron threw Dinky's pointed hat into the darkness. "That is just superstitious gossip and false stories. None of what he said about the knight is true."

Dinky scrambled out to get his hat.

It was a horrible thought, but Rudy had to know, "Are we dead?"

"Of course not! Have you ever heard of a dead person eating

and drinking?" Nipron's voice came out softly. "Don't listen to Dinky. He doesn't know that much about the Knight of Light."

"Do!" Dinky said, entering the tent with his hat.

"Do not!"

"Why can't the Knight of Light just come? Why do you have to invite him?" Billy asked.

"Because the people fear his justice. The knight has a strict code of right and wrong, but stories have been exaggerated. They forget his love and only see the punishment. They don't understand, so they create stories to make the knight out to be someone feared instead of loved.

"Things were getting out of control, so guardians were sent here to take care of problems. When we couldn't solve a problem and needed help, we were the ones that called the Knight of Light," Nipron's voice choked. "Of course, that was before the fire, when there were many guardians."

"Are you a guardian?" Rudy asked.

"He's the only one left!" Dinky straightened his hat. "He's just a young whelp and has a lot to learn, but I'm his helper."

"Pest, that's what you are! My father was a guardian of this land. He died the night the village was destroyed. He and all the other guardians were meeting with the elders at the castle near the village. They were discussing a plan to help the people overcome the evil wizard and correct the thinking of good as evil. It was awful when people started thinking that evil was good and good was evil. It began to destroy the peoples' faith in each other."

"Didn't your father tell you how to find the knight?" Rudy asked.

"He would have. I was being trained to take over his job. I never learned how to contact the knight. It's the last thing I was to learn. There is much to learn, but the most important thing is not to pester the knight with every problem that comes along. My father was only eight hundred years old and had many years yet to complete his task."

"Eight hundred years old?" both Rudy and Billy interrupted.

"That's what I said! He was too young to die. We usually live for thousands of years. That's why I don't know how to contact the knight."

"Why is Dinky so afraid of the knight?" Billy asked.

"Dinky has a good heart, one of the largest among mortals. Unfortunately, because of his size, he is afraid of most things." Nipron patted Dinky's shoulder. "Most mortals have never seen the Knight of Light. People in power made up stories about him and made his justice look cruel and callous. The people became confused when Ratch was teaching them that evil was good and good was evil. He began ever so slowly to change the truth. It's like a small trickle of water eroding sand away until a huge hole of truth is missing."

"So, the people in power were like Ratch?" Billy asked.

"Somewhat, only they were not evil. They were misguided, selfish, and probably controlled by Ratch, but certainly not evil."

Everyone fell silent, busy in their own thoughts. Weary and exhausted from the memories of his father, Nipron told them to get some sleep.

The four lay in the small tent waiting for sleep to come. Rudy shivered as he listened quietly to the breathing of Nipron and Dinky's snores. He couldn't sleep because he kept hearing the cries of the people. Billy tossed and turned thinking about the fires and the destruction of the castle and people.

After a while, they gave up trying to sleep and sat up to talk. Suddenly, they heard a howling wind and saw a deep black darkness come swirling into the tent. A foul rotten egg smell touched their nose.

They gagged and screamed, "Nipron, rotten eggs!" shouted Bill.

Rudy shuddered, "It must be Ratch!"

CHAPTER 6

Light from Nipron's staff shot light toward the black swirls of water as it inched its way toward them. The light flared into ten bright moons then slowed and changed directions. Instead of coming toward them, it rose high in the air.

"The rotten egg smell! It's the Demon of Chaos!" Rudy shrieked.

Black water sizzled and swirled, trying to press forward. It had a life of its own. Nipron's staff touched its edge and a howl of rage erupted. Black waterspouts grew everywhere, twisting and turning, trying to reach out and wrap themselves around everyone.

Nipron's staff flared once again, exploding light and melting the ten moons into one bright light. Suddenly, inside the tent and even the dark sky outside, everything was shown white with light.

The black tendrils quickly withdrew from the tent. Just as quickly, Nipron placed his hands on the ground and said, "Take us from this evil."

The ground trembled and opened its yawning mouth, swallowing them. Rudy felt himself falling and tumbling on and on with the others in the darkness. He was falling so fast that he couldn't see a thing but could only smell the earth. Landing in a heap, Nipron's staff flooded the area with light. The earth had closed behind them as they descended into an enormous cavern. When the staff light snuffed out, Rudy couldn't see anything. Suddenly, light appeared slowly out of the darkness. Overhead he could see thousands of tiny circles glittering like stars. It was as though the earth had never opened to drop them at the bottom of this cavern. The top of the cavern was sealed smooth with thousands of tiny lights from the rocks.

Billy and Rudy wandered around looking at the walls covered in carved images of dwarf warriors—men and women in armor with their swords and hammers. There were many doorways leading from the cavern. A staircase rose above the floor, but it appeared to be a dead end. There was a doorway high above the walkway, but it could not be reached from the stairs. Broken tables displayed signs of daily life, and chairs were upended with chunks missing from them.

Wild-eyed, Rudy's voice croaked, "Was that Ratch? Not that I'm scared, just surprised. It happened so fast!" Taking a deep breath, he looked at his shaking hands.

Climbing over huge boulders, Billy asked, "Is that the same swamp water Ratch used on the village? I can't believe anything can smell that bad!"

"Yes, that was Ratch and his black water." Nipron replied,

looking puzzled. "But how did he find us?"

Billy was already exploring the cave, "Hey, what is this place? What is that walkway that goes halfway up to the top of the cave and just ends with no place to go? How come it doesn't have a handrail? Who carved all those pictures in the walls and table-tops? And where do all those doorways go?"

"Diddly squat! One question at a time. This cavern is eons old, from when there were more of us dwarfs. We used to build cities under the ground. The walkway used to lead to another level. See that doorway up high? That was the way to the outside world. Dwarfs lived in this area at one time. The warriors pictured on the wall were the true defenders of the dwarves. We gave up this area after a fierce battle with the Orcs—and before you ask, Billy—they were created by the Demon of Chaos.

He created them because we kept destroying his serfs. His serfs were dark, and with just a touch of light, they would break you into a million pieces. He needed something that the hammer couldn't freeze. The Orcs had long arms that hung to the ground, with teeth jutting from their lower jaw. Their skin looked as though it had been burned and they were ugly and hateful. They destroyed or tried to destroy everything that we built underground.

There was a great war where we defeated them, but at a great cost. Many died during the battle. Families and young ones were sent to the Blue Mountains. When the war was won, the warriors decided there was too much sorrow in this place and left. We moved to the Blue Mountains to join the others.

This cavern has been abandoned for hundreds of generations."

Rudy really didn't care about the history of the dwarfs or the cavern. He was still shaking and thinking about what would have happened if he and Billy had not been awake. *I don't think I'm ever going to sleep again.* There was something he kept wondering about, so he asked Nipron, "How did the wizard find us?"

"That is a good question, Rudy. He should not have been able to find us, but find us he did." Nipron brushed his scraggly eyebrow and climbed over the large rocks toward one of the dark doorways in the wall. "We need to explore the tunnels to see how to get out of here. I'll take this one and you all start investigating the others."

"Don't you need your light?" Rudy yelled.

Nipron headed into the darkness without answering.

"Nah, he can see in the dark," replied Dinky.

Rudy wished he could see in the dark. He jumped when Dinky thumped him on the back and said, "Thanks to you and Billy, that black water didn't get us. You were really brave."

"Not really, just surprised. Maybe I was afraid, but I'm not sure."

"Dang! Nipron told me it was only a fool that wasn't afraid when there was danger."

"I've never heard that being afraid is okay," Rudy said.

"Sure, it's okay. But there are times when even if you are afraid, you still should do things. I can show you how to maneuver when someone big wants to punch you out. I met a Korean fellow one time from your world. He taught me some great moves. He called it take a dough—no, no—tie quad, no. Diddly squat! What is that called?" Dinky snapped his fingers, "Tae Kwon Do. I'll teach you some moves that you can use anytime."

Rudy thought of Otis and Tank, and how he was always running from them. "I sure could use some moves to help me maneuver around some bullies, but I'm not really afraid of them."

Rolling his eyes, Billy kept quiet.

"Sometimes, people don't realize they are afraid to face their fears," Dinky said quietly.

"Why should you still do things even if you are afraid?" Rudy asked. "If you don't face fear about everyday things, the world becomes a more scary and hateful place. I'm not talking about evil things like Ratch. Anyone in their right mind should be afraid of him. I mean normal everyday fears that a person exaggerates."

"What do you mean, 'normal fears?'" Rudy asked.

"Well Diddly squat! Like, hmmm, let me see, like. . . "

"Like walking over a bridge that you can see through, which is not a bridge at all but a railroad trestle. Or climbing up to a tree house that is ten feet in the air?" Billy asked innocently.

"Yeah, that's it! Unless the bridge isn't safe, or the tree is dead, and the branches will break. Diddly! You've got to use some common sense."

"But I'm so puny. . . " Rudy began.

"Puny? You're bigger than I am. Size has nothing to do with it or I'd be shaking at my shadow! Enough talk, we have to look in the tunnels to find a way out."

Rudy pulled out the big flashlight and followed Dinky and Billy. He handed the flashlight to Dinky as they entered the tunnel. It narrowed, with piles of rocks on each side, until there was nothing but rocks.

"Ok, let's try another tunnel," Dinky said as they turned around.

The next two doorways both led to deadends. In the third one, they were able to walk a long way. Dinky was always some ways ahead of them and they could follow him by the light. Suddenly, Billy and Rudy were swatting at tiny lights that flared on and off, surrounding them.

"Dinky, wait. There are lights attacking us!" Rudy cried.

Dinky quickly swung the flashlight around and began laughing as he walked back toward them. "Stop that swatting. They won't bite, they are just curious."

Billy and Rudy looked at the tiny things in the light and saw that they emitted teeny, tiny flames and smoke. "They're baby dragons," Billy yelled.

"No, they're Dragaletts—the smallest dragons in the world.

They only live in tunnels and caves."

One landed on Billy's' hand. "Will they grow any bigger?"

"Nope. They only get as big as a dragon fly."

"They seem pesky. What good are they?" grumbled Rudy. Suddenly a bunch swarmed around his head. "Okay, okay, sorry. I just asked a question."

"Eons ago, we used them as messengers because they could send messages through rocks by just a thought. Come on, we should head back and try another doorway."

Billy didn't want to leave as several had landed on him and seemed to be content just sitting there. "Can we take them with us?"

"No. Besides, they will not leave the tunnel."

Just a few feet into the next tunnel, rays of colored lights began shooting from the ground to the top of the tunnel. Singing filled the air with words that Billy and Rudy couldn't understand. They just stood and listened. Dinky had walked quite a way into the tunnel before he realized that Billy and Rudy weren't behind him. He turned to hurry back to them and tapped his hammer gently to the floor. The lights and singing disappeared.

"Why did you do that, Dinky? I was enjoying that song and could see people moving in the song.

"Yeah, me too. It was like we were in a movie with the people," said Billy.

"Those were mesmer lights. We used them to stop anyone that was not a dwarf from entering the tunnel. It would stop them and hold them in a trance until we could come and take them prisoner," explained Dinky.

Rudy asked, "Do you think that happened to Nipron? Because he's been gone a long time. Is that why he isn't back?"

Dinky shook his head no. "The Guardians are immune to the different traps that we set. Come on, let's head back to the cavern. This tunnel is a dead end."

They came out of the doorway and Rudy saw a black form shifting, stretching, and then shrinking. It had red eyes that flared like taillights on a car. A shiny, dark creature opened its mouth to show sharp spiked teeth. Claws jutted from its fingertips and bony hooks ballooned from its back.

"Wwwhat is that?" cried Rudy.

"Run!" Billy screamed, pushing Rudy toward the steps. Yelling and running as fast as they could, Rudy and Billy scrambled up the old primitive walkway when suddenly Dinky ran ahead of them. Small rocks crumbled under the steps as the three tried to get away. Rudy looked down. They were up high in the cavern. He was afraid and stumbled and fell on the step. Razor sharp claws were inches from him just as he was able to jump up and continue climbing the steps.

Rudy saw Billy and Dinky standing still, waiting for him. "Run! I'm okay."

They didn't move.

"GO!" Rudy screamed.

"We can't! There are no more steps!!" Billy cried.

Dinky quickly squiggled in front of Bill and Rudy.

A high-pitched howl erupted from the dark form as it slowed its climb and widened its evil smile. The sharp claws clicked in a slow rhythm as the eyes shrank into tiny slits of red glee.

"What are we going to do?" Rudy shrieked. He was scared. Really scared and he knew he was scared.

As the dark form lunged toward them, Dinky pulled his silver hammer from his belt and held it high in the air. The creature stopped in midair and became a statue that could not move. Rudy felt the blistering light before he saw it, flowing into the dark form. He turned and saw Nipron. Light sped from Nipron's fingertips. The light swelled into the dark form until it burst into a million pieces.

"Nipron!" Rudy cried, leaning against the wall with relief. "What was that thing?"

"It was one of the Demon of Chaos' serfs. If he had touched you, well, let's just say, lucky for you he didn't. Now, come on down."

Dinky raced down the steps. Billy was behind him, feeling more than a little queasy. "How did you zap him?"

"Zap him?"

"Yeah, how did you make him break in a million pieces?" Billy asked.

"Oh, that. I just forced light into him, and it destroyed all the dark elements of his form."

"Why did he howl that crazy way?" Billy asked.

"It was a demented cry for help," Nipron replied.

Shaking, Rudy looked down at the bottom of the cave. "How did I get up here? Whew! Not only did I almost die, but now I have to climb down." *Don't think, just don't think.* Rudy kept both hands on the wall as he walked. *Talk and walk. Just talk and walk.* Rudy carefully began the descent, hugging the wall. But his thoughts unnerved him. *What if I slip, or what if the step crumbles?* His hands became slippery with sweat and slid on the wall.

He stopped, sat down, and closed his eyes. "I need to rest a minute and stop shaking." He rubbed his hands on his shorts to get rid of the sweat.

"Rudy," Dinky said in a quiet voice, "you're doing great. You're halfway down. You know it's okay to be afraid. Just sit there until you stop shaking. Then come on down. Just look at the next step, not the bottom of the cave."

Rudy took a deep breath and stood back up. *I am not going to look at the bottom of the cave. I'm not going to think about all the possibilities of what could happen. I'll just look straight ahead at the steps in front of me and take one at a time, one step at a time.* And slowly, step by step, Rudy continued to descend while Dinky and Billy began putting the tent and other items back into the backpack.

Billy asked, "Nipron, how did that thing know we were

here?"

Watching Rudy slowly maneuver down the steps he said, "Yes, how did he know we were here? We were not followed. The Demon of Chaos cannot have eyes everywhere."

Rudy stopped listening to Nipron and sat down on the last step and put his head in his hands. "I've never been so scared in my life. This is being scared. I mean really scared."

"There is nothing wrong with being afraid, nor does it mean you have to give up or not do something when you can." Nipron said quietly as he stared at Dinky. Dinky had finished helping Billy load the backpack and decided to get a snack from Ratch's bag. He opened the food pouch and pulled out a large, smoked turkey and a smoked ham dripping with honey. Still not satisfied, he kept trying and out came two kinds of bread, and many cheeses.

"Dang! Why can't I get any cakes or pies out of this bag?"

Nipron watched Dinky. "Aha, that's it!" Nipron exclaimed as he grabbed the bag from Dinky. "We have to burn this!"

Dinky grabbed the bag back. "Diddly squat! Now I know you're crazy. We need this!"

His scraggly eyebrows knit together, and in a very low voice Nipron said, "Dinky, we need to burn the bag. It must have a following spell. That's why that putrid water came into the tent, and now one of Ratch's serfs found us here. It wasn't by chance! Ratch can tell where we are and sends things to destroy us."

"But what will we do for food?" Dinky whimpered.

"You've pulled enough food out of that bag to last us a long time. Now, give me the bag," Nipron ordered.

Dinky dropped the bag.

Nipron pointed his staff at the bag. A small blue flame ignited and grew to a deep turquoise blue, shooting forward and striking the bag. Flames shot into the bag with an explosion.

CHAPTER 6

Ratch's face had large, welted scars that intersected like lines on a grid. His fire-red eyes glowed at the group. His shadowed face twisted in anger. "You've finally caught on, have you? I will find you again, so be afraid! Be very afraid." Slowly, his face disappeared as the bag turned to ashes.

Rudy stood at the bottom of the cavern, his mouth open and his red frizzy hair standing on end. "I'm never going to make it home."

"Dinky, take care of that food," Nipron ordered.

Dinky wasn't sure what to do. Fortunately, Rudy was able to finally move from the scare of seeing and hearing Ratch. His arms still stiff from fear, he looked like a robot as he pulled out aluminum foil from his backpack and showed Dinky how to wrap the food.

"Amazing! So, we just wrap the food up and it will stay in place? This silver paper is fantastic."

Once the food had been packed securely in Rudy's backpack, Nipron turned to Dinky, "We are in your realm.

The tunnel I found is long, dark, and blocked. We need to find another way out of here. The dwarves must have used the Blufennel to leave this place. Can it still be awakened and used?"

"Of course the Blufennel works." Proudly, Dinky stood as tall as his three feet would allow. "I'll call the Blufennel." Dinky raised the hammer.

"What's the Blufennel?" Billy asked.

Dinky lowered the hammer. "Millions of years ago, the Knight of Light gave the races different gifts to use in our world. The dwarfs chose the Blufennel. It helped us to move from place to place quickly. These legs of ours are so short that it takes us forever to walk anywhere.

The Blufennel is a great blue light that can take us quickly through dirt, stone, and air. This is how our children and families were moved before the Great War. It transported us to a safe place in the Blue Mountains, safe from the Orcs." Standing tall once more, Dinky raised his hammer.

"How do we get into the Blufennel?" Billy asked.

"You do not 'get into' the Blufennel. It wraps itself around you, and in you, and through you. You become one with the Blufennel. As it moves, you will feel that you are stretching and then shrinking. Once we reach our destination, it will release us and go back to sleep until called again," explained Dinky.

Once more, he stood tall and raised his hammer.

"I have just one more question," Rudy said before Dinky could continue. "It almost sounds like a carnival ride. Will we get sick?"

Dinky scrunched up his face, "No, you will not get sick. Carnival smarnrival! Be quiet! Not another word." He brought the hammer down with such force that the bottom of the cavern cracked.

A blue streak of light flew up from the crack and floated around the cavern. A voice whispered like a cat clawing sandpaper, "Who calls the Blufennel?"

Dinky took off his cap, bowed, and said, "It is I, Diddymus of the Stonefoot clan."

The whispered voice asked again, "Are you from the clans at Mist Mountains or the Blue Mountains?"

"Now wait a minute. What difference does it make? You never asked that before."

The Blufenel flew in front of Dinky's face, and in a sharp growling whisper, answered, "The Stonefoot clan has not called on me for eons. Much has changed. The Demon of Chaos tricked me into allowing one of his serfs to use me. It happened only once. It took centuries to heal. It is a good thing that you have not called me until now, for I could not answer."

The Blue streak stood in front of Dinky and pulsed angrily. "I am very cautious about who journeys within me, especially since I have not been called for so long."

Dinky bowed again and said, "I am so sorry. Are we still able to travel with you?"

The Blufennel was quiet for a long time. "If you are specific, I can take you on your journey. Now, which mountains are you from?"

"I am from the Stonefoot clan and the Blue Mountains. I was only a child when we had to move from the Mountains in the Mist."

"Good. Now, where do you wish to go?"

Nipron instructed, "Tell her to take us to the Redooms Valley."

Dinky did as Nipron said, and blue light flooded everywhere, wrapping its rays around each of them, feeling and touching them. Rudy looked at his arms and hands. The blue light seemed to envelope and go right through him. He looked at Billy who was glowing blue. "Billy, am I glowing like you?"

"Yeah, you wouldn't believe how your red hair looks!"

"Hey, we're moving!" Rudy said. He couldn't help but laugh at how the others seemed to stretch and shrink, float and spin. He knew he must be doing the same but didn't feel anything except for the stretching. He felt like he was ten feet tall.

The group abruptly landed on top of a ring of hills overlooking a deep valley. Clapping Dinky on the back, Billy said, "Wow, was that cool or what? How does that thing work? Is it really alive?"

"Of course it's alive!"

"Wow, I'd take that ride again!" exclaimed Rudy. "The only thing I felt was like I was stretching and then shrinking. I didn't even get dizzy when we were spinning. How can something like that be alive, and sleep for eons, and then come awake again?"

Dinky replied, "That is how it was created." He couldn't understand why they were so excited. He had used the Blufennel without giving it a thought for hundreds of years.

Nipron let Rudy and Billy talk on and on about how great the Blufennel was. It wasn't often that Dinky was given such praise. After a time, he pointed to the valley, "This is not the Redooms valley. This is the Valley of Red Blooms."

Nipron stood quiet for quite a long time trying to puzzle things out. "Maybe this valley must be traveled first. Let us venture down into the valley and up the other side. There we will find Redooms."

Everyone looked at where Nipron was pointing. The hills and valleys were deep green with tall grass, though the forest that lined the edge of a large flat rock looked diseased and broken. In the center of the valley, there was a large circle of red.

It was still and quiet without any movement of any kind. No birds, no animals, no crickets chirping. They began to walk toward the red center of the valley when suddenly, the ground began to vibrate, and a low whistling noise rang in their ears. "What's that noise?" Billy asked.

"Stop walking and be quiet," Nipron ordered.

The low whistling sound became louder. Standing still became more difficult because the ground was shaking so fiercely, as though they were standing on a rocking chair that was rocking wildly out of control. Suddenly, a huge yellow worm burst through the earth's surface. It rose over them with feathery yellow wisps curled around each segment of its body. It towered over them, blocking out the sun. Everyone but Nipron was so startled they fell down.

"Aha, Niprrron!" the creature said.

"Clingker! What a great surprise! And just at the right time, too. How great to see you!"

Rudy clutched his chest and gasped for air. *A giant talking worm? What next?*

Nipron continued to talk to Clingker as though he did this every day. He told him all about the Demon of Chaos and the destruction of the healers.

Clingker said, "A great loss, the healers and questors. I don't know what the world is going to do." Sighing deeply, he continued, "You have a great responsibility, but your father prepared you well. He said that you would be one of the great ones."

"Me? My father never told me that. And he also didn't tell me how to call the Knight of Light." Nipron lowered his head into his hands.

"Nipron, I'm sorry I cannot help you. You know I cannot

meddle in affairs above ground. I can see that you are suffering, but you have the strength to complete your task. The knight told you to head north and sent you a key."

"But where in the north? What is the key for? And why give it to someone from another world?"

"I'm sure you will find out all you need to know at the right time. Don't be anxious, just have faith in yourself and what the Knight of Light has told you thus far." Clingker paused, "Make sure you are careful when you enter the woods. I've heard that Dark Knights are roaming in bands. They are burning and plundering the villages. Instead of taking the side of truth, they are encouraging hate and division. They mock truth and make victims of those that they should be helping. They torture them by chaining them to their horses, dragging them behind to race. They bet on who is going to die first." In almost a whisper, he added, "They are not helping the people. Sad, so sad."

Nipron pleaded, "There is no one. Only you and I are left. There must be a way for you to help. You know he is poisoning Lusair."

The worm whistled, "Ahh, I know. Even if I could help, I have no time. You know my job is to try to get rid of that same poison that is also in the soil. Lately, I can't seem to be able to keep up. It's undone as soon as I complete one pass in the soil. Many times I am without sleep as I need to make so many passes."

"Clinker, at least can you tell me if you have seen the Knight of Light? We really need to find him."

"No, not for a long time, but you will find him when you need him most. Of that, I am sure. I must go now. Have faith in yourself." In a flash, he sank into the ground and the whistling sound became distant and low.

"What the heck was that? Billy asked. "What kind of work does he have to do?"

Smiling, Nipron replied, "That was a glowworm! Wherever he goes, the soil gets fed and healed. It is rare to see one that will stop work and take the time to talk to you."

Resuming their journey, they had only taken a few steps when suddenly, Billy felt something grab his foot. He tripped and fell. Immediately, Rudy felt something grab his foot tripped and he tripped and fell. Then Dinky felt something grab his foot and he also tripped and fell!

Billy landed on something soft. He heard an "ooff" sound. He was staring into beady little eyes. Looking up, he saw Dinky's hammer moving on its own and Dinky screaming for someone to bring it back. Stretching out his hand to grab the hammer, a small furry hand pulled his hand down so that he couldn't reach it. Billy pulled away from the tiny hands and jumped up, only to trip again.

He fell down once again, coming face to face with the same beady eyes. This time he saw a hairy, smiling face with a body that was hairy and dirty. Wearing a torn shirt and pants, it looked like a baby pig. But instead of hooves, there were tiny feet and tiny hands.

The creature covered his mouth with matchstick-sized fingers and said, "Shh." Sitting up, Billy saw Rudy laughing so hard he had to take the backpack off and set it on the ground. Dinky was running in circles yelling, "Bring that hammer back to me!" Nipron stood on top of the hill, his face like stone.

The hairy being in front of Billy tugged at his shirt. "My name is Purloin. I'm a Furlet."

"What's a Furlet?" Billy asked.

"I don't know," Purloin answered, scratching some dirt out of his ears. "Me, I guess. Many times, we are called 'pests,' but we are also great heroes in wars." Seeing the puzzled look on Billy's face, he added, "Past wars." And then Purloin disappeared.

Before Rudy could say anything, his backpack suddenly took off and headed down the hill, tiny feet and hands peeking out from the bottom. "Purloin, I told you to leave my backpack alone!" Jumping to his feet, he started to grab the backpack, when he tripped once again.

Purloin grabbed Rudy's collar. Now they were nose-to-nose. "Why are you so rude? I want to talk to you."

Rudy realized that Purloin kept tripping him so he couldn't chase after his backpack. He decided to pick the Furlet up, tucked him under his arm, and ran after the backpack.

Dinky's hammer came into view. In a split second, Dinky grabbed it from the Furlet, and raised it in the air. All motion stopped, and he heard Nipron say, "Dinky, lower the hammer and bring the furlets to me."

Rudy dropped Purloin and picked up his backpack. He followed Dinky, Purloin, and the four other furlets back up the hill. Billy was standing by Nipron grinning, but not daring to laugh.

"Ah, I see Purloin is here. Just what do you think you are doing?" Nipron demanded.

Purloin bowed and graveled before Nipron. "We were only curious about Dinky's hammer and the long boy bag."

"I told you the last time I saw you that it is not a 'long boy bag,' but a backpack. And I also told you to leave it alone," Rudy said.

Dinky went over and thumped Purloin on the head. "There's no reason to steal my hammer!" Raising his voice, Dinky yelled, "You know you're not to even touch this hammer!"

"Steal? Furlets never steal. They just borrow," Purloin insisted

"Diddly squat! I've heard it all."

In a thunderous megaphone voice, Nipron bellowed, "Purloin, you and all the other furlets will leave our possessions alone. By that, I mean you will not touch them! Not a single item!"

Billy jumped at the sound of his voice and whispered to Dinky, "Why is Nipron's voice so loud?"

Dinky whispered back, "Because there are probably 100 furlets hiding in the grass."

Purloin covered his ears, and in a loud squeak said, "O great Nipron, we will follow your command." Purloin bowed and folded his hands in front of him. "O great Nipron."

Frustrated, Nipron shook Purloin and told him to stop it. "If you want to talk, just call me Nipron."

Struggling to stand still after the shaking, Purloin said, "Nipron, you have always been kind to us, so I must warn you about things in the valley. They are sooooooo scary! Things keep popping up out of the ground!"

"What things?" Nipron asked.

CHAPTER 7

"I don't know what popped out of the ground," said Purloin. "It was spooky. It was scary. It was frightening!"

Exasperated, Nipron thumped Purloin on the head. "Can't you just describe what it looked like?"

Scrunching up one eye with his hand on his chin, Purloin said, "Well—let me see—there was a long, long, long black snake with a huge head that would pop up high into the air. Then we would run and hide. It would disappear quickly, but I sure can tell you that it stunk! We had to bury our nose in the dirt because it smelled so rotten."

Rudy wrinkled his nose. *They're probably smelling their own armpits,* he thought.

Nipron replied, "Thank you, Purloin. Now behave and leave our things alone. We are trying to rid Lusair of the Demon of Chaos."

At Nipron's words, four of the furlets instantly disappeared. Purloin shook from head to toe and promised they wouldn't borrow any more of their stuff, and immediately left.

It seemed quiet and still with the furlets gone. The group walked slowly down the hill and into the center of the valley.

"It looks like blood." Rudy said.

"No, those are Red Bells and only bloom in times of sorrow," explained Nipron.

"What do you mean in times of sorrow? Have you had other evil wizards?" Billy asked.

"No, we have not had other evil wizards!" Nipron snapped. "Doesn't your world have times of crisis? Such as when the weather destroys villages, or disease kills much of your population, or dragons appear, burning up the land?"

"Dragons!" both boys yelled.

Nipron sighed, "Not to worry, they haven't been around for a couple hundred years.

"What do you mean? We just got through talking to Sagaious," Billy said. "It would've been great to have seen him breathe fire."

"Diddly squat! You wouldn't want to be around when he was spewing that liquid flame all around!" Dinky replied. "Besides, Sagacious is a special kind of dragon. He doesn't go around burning everything up. Most times, he has his head in the clouds."

"Enough about dragons. As I was explaining, the red bells only bloom when Lusair is in trouble." Nipron said.

Billy asked, "Well, why is this the first time we are seeing them?"

"Because they can choose to bloom where there is danger."

Billy and Rudy stopped. "Danger, what kind of danger?" they both asked at once.

"The kind Purloin was talking about. Something unknown, so we must be very careful," said Nipron.

"What's the black circle in the middle of that field?" Rudy asked.

Nipron didn't have time to answer. The black spot rose like a giant snake, straight up into the sky. Nipron threw himself flat on the ground and told the others to do the same.

They all fell face down, except Rudy, who tripped and whirled around and fell on his back. His eyes bugged out and a silent scream came from his mouth. Digging his fingers into the soil, he wanted to close his eyes, but couldn't.

The huge, snake-like object whipped and twirled back and forth, up and down. A mouth slowly opened and closed with gleaming metal levers inside. Its huge eyeball whirled and hummed when it shifted near them, as though it was searching, searching—for them. It came right over them and hovered forever. At least that's how long it felt to Rudy. He thought he saw red eyes in the open mouth, but it was twirling so fast he wasn't sure.

The huge swirling eyeball careened past them again. Its pupil brightened and then dimmed to a thin gleam of light that pulsated and throbbed. Rudy's throat was so tight it was impossible to swallow. He wanted to cup his hands over his ears to block the whirring noise, but he couldn't move. The long spindly neck suddenly disappeared. Everyone lay still for a long time. Rudy finally asked, "Why didn't that thing see us? It was right on top of us forever!"

"I asked the ground to shelter and hide us, and that's what it did. I need to get closer to see if I can figure out what that thing is," Nipron said.

Dinky grabbed Nipron's leather coat. "No, it has to be the Demon of Chaos' lookout."

"Wait here," Nipron ordered.

Turning over onto his stomach, Rudy stared for a long time at the field filled with red. Tears came to his eyes. The flowers were so brilliant and beautiful, yet so sad. He inched closer to Dinky and asked, "Can you see Nipron? He's been gone a long time."

Dinky stood up and looked at the meadow. The black thing was gone. Nipron was gone. "I think we better try to find him."

They all stood up and started slowly walking, step by step, close together. They reached the middle of the flowers.

"There's nothing here but flowers, and more flowers." Billy gently kicked at the tops of the flowers. "How could something that big not leave a trace? And where's Nipron?"

"Diddly! You're right. If we hadn't seen that thing, I wouldn't believe anything had been here." Looking around,

Dinky pointed to the large flat rock. The rock was three feet above the flowers, surrounded on the back side by trees. "Let's head there and see if we can see anything else."

A distant rumble quivered under their feet. Dinky yelled, "Run! Run for your lives!"

They ran like scarecrows out of control. Their arms jerked back and forth as they tried to keep their balance. The ground shifted under their feet and caused them to bend forward and then backward. They were almost to the rock when Rudy fell. Billy stopped and grabbed Rudy's hand as a swoosh of air exploded through the ground so great that it pushed them both onto the rock.

The long, black, snake-like thing with its giant eyeball burst to the surface, spewing chunks of dirt everywhere. As quickly as the eyeball appeared, it sank and disappeared.

Rudy whispered in Dinky's ear, "How did you know the rock was a safe place?"

"Lucky guess."

Billy moved closer to Dinky and whispered, "How come it didn't see us here?"

"Even if it has an eyeball, I don't think it can see." Dinky sat and rubbed his wrinkled face. "Dang, it must have felt us walk on the ground. Once we got on the rock, it couldn't feel us anymore."

Rudy looked at the rock under his feet. "Are you sure?"

"No! Diddly squat! You have to use a little common sense

once in a while. That eyeball was so high in the sky that it could see for miles!" said Dinky.

"What do we do now?" Rudy asked. Dinky started pacing, "I think we'll stay here until morning. Maybe Nipron will be back, if not we'll follow that path." Dinky pointed to a worn trail that led into the forest at the edge of the rock.

Rudy felt as though he had to do something before he started shaking again. He didn't feel safe pitching the tent on the ground and he couldn't pound the stakes into the rock. *I'll spread the tarp out so that we can have something to lay on tonight.* He was careful not to shatter the quiet that seemed to envelope them. He quietly took the tent and slowly spread it out.

Billy had been standing at the edge of the rock, looking out, trying to find the black eyeball, but with no luck. He turned his head and saw Rudy struggling with the tent. Turning to head over to help straighten out the tent, he slipped off the rocky ledge and sunk into the red flowers. The large black mouth burst through the flowers and quickly sucked Billy into its mouth.

Billy was gone.

"AGGG!" Dinky cried, clutching his heart.

Rudy turned and rushed to Dinky, "What's the matter?

"The thing—it got Billy!" Dinky yelled.

"What?" screamed Rudy. Running to the edge, ready to plunge into the red flowers, he felt Dinky grab his leg and stop him.

"Don't leave this rock!" Dinky cried. "Billy fell off the rock and that thing swallowed him faster than you could draw a breath."

Looking wildly at Dinky, and then the place where Billy disappeared, Rudy didn't know what to do. He began to run around in a circle, clutching his hair, and sobbing loudly. His friend, his lifelong friend, was gone. Billy, who always protected him. "Gone, gone, what am I going to do?"

Dinky stood up as the rock began to shake. "Rudy, don't lose heart. . . Agggggggg!"

"Dinky! Dinky!" Rudy leaped toward him. As Dinky was falling off the rock, the eyeball opened its mouth with gleaming metal teeth, rose, and then captured Dinky. Rudy tried to grab his foot but missed by a gnat's whisker.

"Noooooooooooo!" The sound echoed all around him. He lay still, his hand outstretched. The only sound he heard was the pounding of his heart. He lay there till the sun began its descent. Suddenly, the ground quivered and Rudy sat up. He watched the last thin rays of the sun disappear behind the mountain.

Okay, now let's think this through. That eyeball isn't coming back if I stay on the rock. I'm in a weird land. I don't know where I am, and don't know where to go. My best friend is gone and the only ones that know what this land is all about are gone. Rudy stood up, raised his fist in the air, and shouted, "I'm afraid! Boy, am I afraid!"

71

His voice echoed back again and again, and then silence surrounded him. Pacing, he muttered to himself, "I've been scared about everything, every day of my life. What a dork. I couldn't even climb a dumb tree." Rudy laughed. "That serf was a whole lot scarier than those guys who wanted me to walk the bridge. Billy's right, how could I've been so dumb?" *Where is Billy?*

Rudy swallowed hard and rubbed his neck. He felt the chain and the key. He rubbed it without thinking. A light began to glow, catching his eye. Quickly, he pulled the chain over his frizzy hair and dropped it on the ground.

The sphere-shaped light grew more intense and chased the darkness away. In the center of the circle stood the Knight of Light. His white hair glistened in the light. "You've taken your first step, Rudy. You've admitted your fear. Now you must overcome it. Do not be too afraid in this strange world. Your key will protect you and aid in your quest. Your friends are alive, but you must find your courage and free them."

"But where are they?" Rudy asked.

The Knight of Light continued as though Rudy had not spoken. "Your answers will be found in the north. Take care of the key. It will protect you. No one can take it from you, you have to freely give it. Tell Nipron he has the knowledge to save the world. He just has to use it." In a softer voice the Knight said, "Have faith in yourself, Rudy."

The light vanished. Rudy grabbed the key and desperately rubbed it again and again and again. Nothing happened. Frustrated, he put the chain back over his head and sat on the tent. Sighing deeply, he thought, *At least Billy and the others are still alive, now I just have to find them.* Though the sun had set, there was still a soft glow of light peeking through the darkness. The Red Bells glowed in the dark, preventing the night from turning pitch black

How in the heck am I supposed to find them? Why can't the Knight of Light just show me where they are? What if they are hanging in a bag off the cliff? What if I can't find them? I have no idea where they are! Consumed by his thoughts, Rudy moaned. Lying down, he felt the ground tremble around him. But instead of being afraid, he fell into a deep sleep.

Rudy woke up alone, lost in a strange land. The stillness invaded his ears. The only sound he heard was— nothingness. The quiet enveloped and froze his movements, cutting short his breathe. After sitting for a long while, he took his compass out of the backpack. Looking at the compass, he moved it until it pointed north. The worn path was the way to go. *If I step off this rock onto the path, will that black thing finally get me? If I stay here on the rock, it is safe. But how would I find Billy? I just have to do it!* He bent over and packed the tent. Picking up his backpack, he continued walking into the woods, slipping the compass into his pocket.

A mist rose, shrouding the sunlight in hazy strips of light. Fog gave the trees a dark shadowy appearance, the branches reached out as if to touch him as he passed by. Large black rocks materialized suddenly among brush and vines. A couple of times, Rudy's heart leaped into his throat because some of the rock shapes were tall and looked like a person standing along the side of the path. The silence continued, with only the swishing sound of branches rubbing across his backpack.

Suddenly, a group of knights appeared out of the mist. Their armor was tarnished, and their horses' manes and tails were ragged and tangled. "Here, boy! What are you doing in these woods?"

"I'm looking for. . . "

"Look!" One of the younger knights pointed at Rudy. "Where did you get that?"

"What?" Rudy asked in a hushed voice.

The older knight said, "The key! You must have stolen it! Hand it over. Ratch has been searching for that for months."

Rudy lifted the necklace as if to give it to the Knight—stalling to give himself time to think. *Ratch? He's the bad guy. Nipron said the knights were under a spell and didn't know right from wrong. Things aren't right here. Nipron also told us that sometimes we have to go with our gut feeling.* Rudy made his decision, "No," he said. "The Knight of Light gave it to me and told me to give it to Nipron."

Howling with rage, the knight raised his hands, and from his fingertips black lightning shot out everywhere.

Bright light and fire erupted all around Rudy, as he cowered and hugged himself. *I'm done for*, he thought. He felt his clothes heating up from the crackles of the lightning and smelled something burning. *My hair is probably fried.*

When the lightning subsided, he opened his eyes, quickly feeling his hair and clothes. *I'm still all in one piece!* Without giving the knight another look, he raced into the woods. Tree branches lashed at his face and vines grabbed at his feet, causing him to fall. Half crawling and half running over wet boulders, he didn't even feel the mist that washed over him like rain. Sounds of the knights grew closer as they maneuvered their horses through the thick growth of trees. It felt as though all the woods were trying to trap him, reaching out, clinging to his hair and clothes as he twisted and turned to avoid trees and vines.

Finally, he could run no farther and tripped, falling into a heap. The drumming noise he heard was his heart pounding in his ears. Gasping for breath, and his chest heaving, Rudy looked back. He had lost them.

Holding the key, he said, "The knight was right, this protected me. Whew! I could've been a pile of ash by now."

All at once, a lone black knight on horseback stood in front of him. "You will give the key to me. Now."

CHAPTER 8

Rudy tried to stand but slipped and fell in front of the horse's hooves. The horse reared up and then came straight down, aiming right at his head. Just when he thought it was over, something latched onto his feet and pulled him quickly through the brush. The horse came down hard, stumbled, unseating the knight who fell and hit his head on a rock, knocking him out.

Now that he didn't have to worry about horse hooves, Rudy tried to stop whatever was pulling him. But he was being pulled too fast. He tried to grab a hold of tree branches, vines, rocks—whatever he could find. He would have his hand almost wrapped around something, when whatever was pulling him would speed up. Coming to a clearing, the pulling finally stopped.

Groaning, he sat up and looked around. In front of him was tiny, dirty, Purloin. "How could something as small as you pull me all this way and so fast?!"

"Because there were a hundred of us pulling you."

"Where are they all?"

Purloin ignored the question. "Boy, that horse almost had you! One more second and your brain would've been mush." Purloin was quiet for a few minutes. Frowning, he put out his hand. "You know, you need to reward your hero."

"Are you a hero? Or someone that expects a reward for doing good?" Purloin ran up into Rudy's lap, grabbed Rudy's collar, and pulled him nose to nose. "Are you making fun of me?"

Rudy struggled and finally pushed Purloin off from him. "Of course not. You do remember what Nipron told you?"

"Yesssssss!" Purloin said. "I won't borrow anything from your long boy pack."

"It's a backpack!"

Ignoring Rudy's correction, Purloin looked around and asked, "Where is Nipron?"

Rudy shook his head, "I don't know. Billy and Dinky were swallowed by that black thing you saw in the field and told us about. Nipron must have been swallowed too because he just disappeared."

Purloin put his hand over his heart and staggered. "Nipron is dead. . . "

"NO, no! The Knight of Light came and told me to go find them. They are NOT dead!" Rudy yelled.

Purloin closed one eye and put his hands on his hips, not sure if he believed Rudy or not. "The Knight came to see you? He doesn't just come to see anyone, you know!"

"I know, I know. That's what Nipron said." Rudy repeated what the Knight had told him. "And by the way, thank you for saving my life.

Purloin's face broke into a smile, "Okay! Where's my reward?"

Rudy couldn't help but laugh. Purloin did deserve a reward. He took his backpack off and looked inside. Or *tried* to look inside. Purloin kept attempting to climb in and grab things.

"Hold on," Rudy said as he pulled out a small magnifying glass. "I really don't have a good reward. . . "

Purloin grabbed the magnifying glass and squealed with delight. He turned it over and over in his hand and then looked at Rudy, yelled, dropped it, and hid his eyes with his hands.

Puzzled, Rudy asked, "What happened? Why are you covering your eyes?"

"If I cover my eyes, you can't see me. I don't like wizards. Especially ones that grow larger when I look through the clear rock."

Laughing, Rudy pulled Purloin's tiny hands down from his face. "I'm not a wizard. I'm a boy from another world. That is not a clear rock, it's glass that makes things bigger." Gently, he took Purloin's hand and showed him how large it looked under the glass. Purloin couldn't believe it! He looked through the glass, then at his hand. Grabbing the magnifying glass, he looked at his tiny feet. Then the button on his raggedy pants, then a leaf, then a rock, then a tree—

he kept looking and walking.

Rudy smiled at his retreating hero. *It feels good to be with someone that made me laugh and who didn't try to kill me!*

After a few minutes, he remembered the Dark Knights and quickly moved on. Looking around at the shadows in the mist, he pulled the compass out of his pants pocket. Carefully placing the compass on a rock, the arrow pointed north. Grabbing the compass and running, he came to the end of the woods, face to face with a steep mountain wall of rocks that rose into the sky. *Now what am I supposed to do? I was afraid of climbing a couple steps to my tree house! A mountain goat would have problems with this pile.*

Placing his foot in a crevice and lunging for a rock above him, he began climbing. His foot slipped. *Hang on, hang on. No time to panic.* Slowly, he pulled himself up and found another crevice for his foot. "Stretch, all I have to do is stretch," he grunted, until he came to a ledge and pulled himself up. Once on top of the ledge, he lay still and looked down. "I've never been so high off the ground in my life!"

His eyes trailed to the top of the mountain and spotted a cave just a little way up. Rudy got up and started again. He twisted and turned as he grabbed at rocks. At the opening of the cave, Rudy held the compass. It pointed north, into the mouth of the cave. He walked into the dark cave and saw that it went straight through to the other side. Continuing to walk slowly, he saw Billy, Dinky, and Nipron! They were sitting in a line with their hands and feet bound by a thick rope.

"Billy! You're here!! I thought you were a goner—until the

Knight of Light told me you were still alive. I thought I would never see you again. How'd you guys get in here!"

"Rudy!" Billy cried, as Rudy ran to untie him. He jumped up and they grabbed each other. "I didn't think I'd ever see you again!"

"Ahem, would you two mind untying us first?" Nipron asked.

"Nipron, did you hear me? The Knight of Light came to see me."

Dismayed, Nipron asked, "Again?"

"Yes, I rubbed this key. Remember he gave it to me in the woods? Well, it started to glow, and he appeared." He continued to untie Nipron.

"You mean he told you we were in this cave?"

"No, he told me to go north." Rudy quickly told them about the other knights, especially the one that threw black lightning.

"A Dark Knight that throws black lightning is one of the Demon of Chaos workers. Like Ratch is one of his workers, except Ratch is alive," Nipron said.

"You mean that knight was dead?" Rudy asked.

"Yes, the knight was from the underworld. Only someone from the underworld can throw black lightning."

Rudy felt weak and slumped against the wall. "At least it

didn't hurt me."

"Thanks to the key," Nipron said softly. "That must be why the eyeball didn't snatch you. It couldn't find you. You say all you had to do was rub the key and the Knight of Light appeared?"

"No, it doesn't work like that anymore. I've tried many times. I don't know why it worked then. Who was in the eyeball?" Rudy asked.

"No one. Just us, and a bunch of levers," Dinky said, as Billy finally untied the last knot and set him free.

"Well, who tied you up?"

Billy answered, "We don't know. One minute we were in the eyeball, and the next minute we were all tied up."

"But why did it pick you up and dump you here?"

"I've been thinking about that." Nipron scratched his ear. "Ratch could have just as easily gotten rid of us, once and for all. It must be the key that he needs, and he knew you'd come looking for us."

"The knight said no one can take it from me. I would have to give it to them," Rudy said.

"Dang! That won't stop Ratch. He has ways that would make you want to give it to him," Dinky said.

"Stop it, Dinky. Come on, we have to get out of here quickly," said Nipron.

"Where are we going?" Billy asked.

"To the Guardian Keep. If the Knight of Light won't come to me, then I have to find answers elsewhere." Nipron quickly walked away.

Rudy felt guilty because Nipron wanted to see the knight, and he was the one that ended up talking to him. "The Knight said you didn't need him. He said you have all the answers and to have faith in yourself."

"If I have all the answers, why don't I know it?" Nipron walked ahead of them. The only sound they heard was the flapping of his leather coat.

In no time, they came to the end of the cave and saw sand dunes as tall as mountains. There were rows and rows of tan-colored piles of sand standing as though guarding secrets of long ago. The sunlight streamed across the hills altering color from white, to tan, to dark brown. "Look to the center of the dunes. Look hard and you will see a lake. That is the Guardian Keep," said Nipron.

They looked hard at the hills. Squinting, Rudy asked, "What lake?"

Narrowing his wrinkled eyes, Dinky cried, "I see it! See that little speck of blue?"

"Come on. It will take the rest of the day to get there," Nipron said.

"The rest of the day? How about the rest of the week? That speck of blue is a hundred miles away," said Billy.

Dinky replied, "Not to worry. I saw Nipron point at our feet. We'll be making double time today,"

Climbing down the mountain of rocks, and walking for hours in slippery sand, the small group did not tire. Every step they took forward, the loose sand didn't send them back, but instead sent them forward again! At times, they were on their hands and feet crawling, sliding over the hills of sand. They came to the edge of the lake as the last of the sun rays caught its brilliant blue-green shimmers.

"Wow! What did you do, Nipron? We sure got here faster than I would have dreamed possible," Billy said.

"It's called a two-step. For every one step you take, it doubles your step and then doubles your step again. We made it in double-double time," said Dinky.

They were tired and stood watching the birds flutter in the water on the peaceful lake that was as blue as the sky. They watched Nipron as he stood at the edge of the lake with his arms spread wide. "Oh, Keeper of Truth, let your child come in."

A shimmering door appear in front of the lake. Just a door. No walls—just a door.

Billy blinked his eyes. "Let's go," Nipron said, as he opened the door.

Rudy and Billy hesitated to walk through a wall of sand, even if there was a door. Dinky finally pushed them inside. The room was immense, with a soft bluish-glow casting wavy shadows everywhere. The floor was large, with white shells like tiles that fit perfectly, making the floor smooth as glass. The high, arched ceiling shimmered with different hues of blue, as the wave movement sounded like a distant drum beating in a slow rhythm.

Astounded to see a fish swim by in the ceiling, Rudy cried, "We really are under the lake."

Billy's eyes bulged with excitement. "Yikes! look at the size of that pike. Boy, would I love to have my fishing pole now!"

Nipron ignored the others and walked to the center. On the smooth shell-covered floor was a replica of the chain and key that Rudy wore, engraved in gold. A large white shell was a short way away with bubbling water falling into a small pool filled with sea grass.

Nipron quietly muttered a few words. The circle of chain rolled back, revealing an oblong space from which a wall of books rose high into the air. Rudy stood with his mouth open as Nipron floated to the middle of the wall and wrestled the largest book off the shelf and then floated down and began reading.

"Wow! Can we learn to do that?" Billy asked.

"Hey, come over here," Dinky cried. "Look!"

Billy hurried to Dinky's side. Rudy had a hard time tearing himself away from watching Nipron. He walked backwards with his eye on Nipron until he bumped into something soft. "Wow! A horse with wings I didn't see you when we came in. How did you get here? I mean I know you flew, but how did. . . "

The majestic animal bowed his head to drink in the soft bubbling pool of water. Proudly raising his head, shaking its thick gold ringed mane and tail, he said, "I come and go as I please. How doesn't matter."

"In our world—" Rudy stammered, surprised to find himself talking to a flying horse, "in our world, horses don't have wings or talk."

The winged horse ignored Rudy and asked Dinky, "What are you doing here? You know that mortals have never been here."

In awe of meeting the winged horse, Dinky softly stammered, "Dang, better ask Nipron that."

The winged horse ran around the wall. "Nipron! Is it really you?"

Nipron looked up with a frown until he saw his old friend. He put down the book and ran to greet him. Nipron and Pega touched foreheads. "Oh, Pega, where have you been? I've missed you and need your help desperately."

Pega nudged Nipron, "I thought you were lost in the fire. I did not know you were still alive. I'm sorry about your father. He was a great leader."

Nipron gulped. "I miss him terribly. I feel so useless. I can't even find the Knight of Light. Have you seen him?"

"Not for a long time."

Rudy, Billy, and Dinky crowded around to listen.

Nipron continued, "I know that we do not allow mortals in here, but these are desperate times. The Knight of Light gave Rudy the key."

"I wondered how he got it. Your father used to wear one all the time," Pega said.

"He did? I remember seeing him with a key, but I didn't know he always wore it." Nipron shook his head wearily. "The Knight told Rudy that we didn't need him, that I have the knowledge to stop Ratch. But I don't. I don't know what he meant! That's why I came here. Do you have any idea what he was talking about?"

Pega lowered his head and rubbed it against his foreleg. "Is that why you were reading?"

"A lot of good it did me. I need more information. There are a dozen Guardian keeps filled with knowledge and books, but they are scattered all over Lusair. I don't have time to go to them all. The books here talk of passageways to different worlds. And 'light.' A guardian needs a great deal of light to send darkness away. I know I can destroy Ratche's serfs that way by filling them with light, but to make all the darkness go away, that would take a tremendous light. That kind of light, I don't have."

Pega looked at the shelves of books. "Are these all the books stored in this keep?"

Exasperated, Nipron placed the book he was holding back on the shelf. He placed his hand on the shelf and saw a picture of a water fountain. Staring at the small picture he said, "I don't know of any others—wait a minute." Walking over to the water fountain, he put his hand into the pool and pulled out a book. "I'd almost forgotten about this one. When I was young my father told me if anything happened to him, I must come here and read this. That small picture of the fountain reminded me."

Nipron didn't say a word. He read. Tears filled his almond-shaped eyes as his hands covered his face. "My father knew he was going to die, and that the village was going to be burned." Wiping the tears away, his voice cracking, Nipron said, "He knew. He knew they would try to destroy the healers. But they didn't! Pega, my father saved the healers. It just appeared that they died.

But they didn't."

CHAPTER 9

Nipron bowed his head and sobbed. Slowly, the sobbing stopped. "My father was a true hero. He used the last of his magic to transport the healers away from the fire. The only problem was that he couldn't transport himself."

"There's hope, then?" Rudy asked.

"Yes, yes," Nipron whispered. "It was foretold that some healers would escape." He rushed over to Pega and whispered, "It's a fact. They are hidden and will stay hidden until Ratch is sent back."

Pega nuzzled Nipron. "I know. There was a group of young questor guardians, also. You won't be alone, Nipron. You will be their teacher. I have them safely hidden away."

Slowly, the impact of Pega's words sunk in. He looked at the books and said, "With all the Guardian keeps and their books, I'll not only be teaching but learning for eons!"

Rudy had a question that was bothering him. He interrupted, "How come your father was able to save the healers and the other questors? I thought they were all unconscious?"

"You're right, Rudy. My father wrote that he didn't drink anything in the castle that day, nor did he let the younger guardians. The older ones drank the water and the wine and told my father he was being paranoid. He had enough time to save the others, but not himself, and to send this book here. He was a great hero. He said that Ratch could be sent back."

Before he could say anything, else, Dinky asked, "Dang, send Ratch back where?"

"Back to the Demon of Chaos. Ratch is his servant." Nipron said.

Rudy could feel the chill of Nipron's words. He hated the quietness that settled like a fog over the group. "But how can Ratch be sent back?"

"By us!" Nipron said.

Running his hand through his red frizzy hair, Rudy said, "I was afraid you were going to say that."

"Just how do you propose we do that?" Dinky snapped.

"Did the book tell you how we're supposed to do this?" Billy asked.

"Not exactly." Nipron responded.

"Did it tell you where we're supposed to send Ratch back?" Rudy asked.

"Not exactly."

"Did it tell you anything about what we're supposed to do?"

Pega asked.

"Not exactly."

"Dang! Exactly what did the book say?" Dinky asked.

"That we need the key from the Knight of Light in order to open the passageways between the different worlds."

Everyone looked at Rudy. He felt red creep around his ears as he asked, "Am I supposed to do something?"

Nipron replied, "Not exactly. The book ends too soon. The key is only found in the Guardian's care and no one else's. But I do know when I'm going to use the key."

"Maybe we should stay here until we figure it out," Rudy urged. "It seems really safe here."

"Like we can help by sitting under a lake," Dinky snorted.

"It's not a bad idea. I do need time to sort things out. We have to try to figure out a plan," Nipron said.

"It seems to me the key may help you find Ratch. It helped Rudy find all of you," said Pega.

"The key didn't help. The Knight of Light told me the answers are in the north," Rudy heard himself saying.

"Then let's get started. I can think and sort things out as we go," Nipron said.

"Wait a minute!" Dinky said. "So, we head north. Dang! Then what?"

"Well—if we run into trouble, the key will protect us," Rudy said.

"You! But what about the rest of us?" Billy asked. "Remember that thing snatched us, not you!"

"Well—when there's danger, crowd around me."

Dinky wasn't so sure the key would shield all of them. "Nipron, give it a test."

"A test? What are you talking about?"

"Yeah, use your lightning. Try to zap Rudy," Dinky said. "Then if you can't hit him, try to zap us when we touch him."

"Have you gone mad? If your little experiment doesn't work, you could end up dead," warned Nipron.

Rudy looked at Dinky and shook his head. He felt his knees buckle. *Zap me with lightning?*

"Dang! Nipron, just put it on low zap voltage. The worst that could happen is that we'll be knocked out for a while," said Dinky.

"Is this going to hurt?" Billy asked.

Pega tossed his head. "Actually, it's not a bad idea."

Exasperated, Nipron pointed and threw lightning at Rudy, but it couldn't touch him. He tried again with no success. Dinky grabbed Rudy's knee. Nipron tried to hit them both but couldn't touch either of them. Billy linked his arm through Rudy's. Nipron could not hit any of them with his lightning.

"Looks like it will work," Pega said.

"Okay, okay, so we can't be touched if we hold on to Rudy. So, we head north," said Dinky. Squeezing his wrinkled face so tight it turned purple he asked, "Dang! What do we do once we get there?"

They heard a roar, and the ceiling cracked. Water began pouring onto them.

"It must be Ratch! We have to get out of here!" Nipron yelled.

"Quick, this way!" Pega yelled.

They raced past the fountain into clouds. "We're running through fog. It's so thick I can't see," Billy cried.

"Everyone, grab each other's hands, and Nipron, grab my tail," instructed Pega.

"Wow, it feels like we're flying while standing still. I can feel the wind whistling in my ears," said Rudy.

They stopped far away from the sand and lake and were nearing a forest. The sun had set, and darkness had settled in. The full moon seemed to be the brightest one they had ever seen.

"I must go," said Pega.

Nipron didn't want to see him leave. "I had hoped you could go with us, Pega."

Lowering his head and nuzzling Nipron's hand, he said, "Ah, old friend. You know I can't go with you. Right now, I must go and make sure that some very special people are still safe."

"You know where they are?" Nipron gasped.

"Hush, Nipron. We don't know what ears are about. Know this—we will be together in the north." Pega flew swiftly into the dark moonlit night, his wings beating like a hundred eagles overhead.

The moon was as bright as day, so they could easily move about. They hurried down the knoll quietly in the moonlight. Nipron saw an outcrop of rocks. "Let's look for shelter over there," he said.

The rock formation made a roof for their shelter. The sand underneath made a comfortable bed. Rudy lay his head on his backpack and heard the ground rumble.

"What's that?" Dinky asked.

"It's probably the eyeball looking for us," Rudy said through a yawn.

Billy was grinning at Rudy. "Rudy, you're not afraid. You really aren't afraid!"

"Before you get too comfortable Rudy, I need to show you those moves when someone wants to beat you up," Dinky said.

Rudy didn't want to learn any moves. He was tired from the day. But then he thought of Tank and Otis. Getting up, he slowly walked to a clearing with Dinky.

Dinky had a hard time convincing Rudy to attack him, but once he did, Rudy found himself on his back or face in the dirt many times. "Remember to stay calm and don't get mad. Just practice the moves I'm showing you. Once you get the hang of moving your whole body in rhythm, it will come easy."

While Dinky was talking, Rudy thought he would surprise Dinky with a move of his own. But Dinky was ready and flipped Rudy on his back once again.

Groaning, Rudy said, "I need a lot more practice IF I can survive being flipped every which way." Standing up and walking away he said, "That's it for tonight. I need to rest." Returning to his backpack, he laid down and immediately fell asleep.

The next morning, they walked north. The air left a frosty haze that flecked trees with marks of white. Rudy, compass in hand, led the small group, trudging through fields of wintered grass that were long and mustard colored. Signs of deer and other small animals were evident as grass had been eaten and moved to build small shelters. There were no fences, just markers showing who owned the land. Soon they came to other fields that were barren as there were no deer or birds or small animals.

They eventually entered a gnarled grove of old dying fruit trees. Nipron told everyone to stop. He pulled Rudy over to a moss-covered log and sat him down. "I want you to tell me exactly what the Knight of Light said to you. Both times.

Take your time and leave out nothing."

Rudy sat on the log, trying to remember his first encounter. "The Knight said I had to overcome fear and that I had just entered Kneelgrove."

Nipron yelped, "You never told me that!"

"I guess not. I thought you knew what world you lived in."

"They call our world Lusair. Kneelgrove must be a passageway from your world into Lusair. Not the name of our world!"

"So that's how I got here?"

Nipron said, "The key, the key—what else?"

"That I should have faith in myself and the key would protect me."

"Need the key—enter the passageway—faith in yourself—protects. Go on, go on," Nipron muttered.

Rudy tried to think carefully of the exact words. "He said the key would help in our quest. He also told me that you don't need him. You have the answers and know where to head north."

"Okay, it is starting to make sense. I must think this through a bit more. Lead on with your compass."

The others quietly followed him. Leaving the grove, the air turned colder and soon they trudged over a barren plain. There was nothing as far as one could see but frozen, cracked land. The small group walked closer together, while lonely howling noises swept over the vast plain. Large white flakes of snow began to fall heavily. The wind blew swirls of snow onto them. Their clothes turned white, and they looked like walking snowmen. It was a struggle to continue on.

Nipron stopped. "I have it!" Through the swirling snow, he looked at Rudy and said, "The key is the answer! You need the key to enter the passageway."

Shivering and stomping his feet Rudy asked, "The one I'm wearing?"

"Yes! The Knight of Light gave it to you and that's how you got into our world, Lusair."

Dinky's teeth chattered. "Dang! Can you use the key to go to other worlds?"

"I wish we could use it now. I'm freezing in this one!" Billy said.

Nipron nodded as he watched them shiver and stamp their feet. Suddenly, he realized that they were covered with snow and were cold. "Sorry, I wasn't paying attention. You must be freezing." He waved his hands and the snow disappeared from their clothes. He pulled warm hooded robes out of his pockets for them to wear.

"Thanks, Nipron. I was beginning to think I was going to freeze to death. Hey, I didn't have a key to enter Lusair." Billy said.

Nipron thought for a moment. "You must have been close

enough to Rudy to be able to enter when the gateway was wide open. Remember, Pega said my father had such a key and always wore it around his neck. I didn't have a key, so the Knight of Light sent it to you!"

"Does that mean you want me to give you the key?" Rudy asked.

"Not yet," Nipron said quietly. "There will come a time when I may need your key. After a pause, Nipron asked. "Would you be able to give it to me without an explanation?"

"What if he needs it to protect us when you want it?" Billy asked.

Nipron rubbed the top of his bald head. "That may just be when I need it."

"Nipron would never put you in danger," Dinky said, "not on purpose. It would have to be really important. He'd have something figured out so we could get away."

Nipron's eyes were the saddest they had ever seen. "I would never sacrifice your life for mine. But Dinky is right. You may have only your courage to protect you when I need the key."

"I don't know. It's scary to think about," Rudy said. "But yeah, I'll try and give you the key. I don't believe you would ask for it if you didn't really need it."

Silence hung over the small group as they continued to walk through the barren snow-covered land. Rudy enjoyed the warmth of the robe. It felt like it had just come out of a dryer.

He wondered if he would be able to give the key to Nipron. *I'm not afraid of my own shadow anymore, but this world seems full of dangerous things. I've done things I've never thought possible, even if I was afraid. Maybe it won't be too hard to give Nipron the key when he needs it.*

Rudy felt small and vulnerable and started talking to no one in particular. "I feel like we are tiny ants scurrying across this empty land."

"Yeah, I've never seen so much white before. No trees, no house, no shadows, nothing! It sure is spooky," Billy said.

"Are you afraid, Billy?" Rudy asked.

"Sure am! But we gotta keep on going. I figure it's the only way we can get back home. When Nipron beats the demon, then he can help us find the passageway home," Billy said.

"What if Nipron doesn't win?" Rudy asked.

"Quit borrowing trouble. You are always doing that. Just because you're scared, you make things worse than they are. Forget the 'what ifs.' Nipron has a plan. Have faith in him," Billy said.

"And don't forget yourself—have faith in yourself," Dinky added.

"Okay, okay, you're right. I do borrow trouble. I'll stop! And, you are right, I need to have faith. I'll stay strong!" Rudy said. Hunching his shoulders and muttering to himself he added, "I've got no choice, no choice at all."

Trees began to dot the landscape and soon a dark, disease-ridden forest loomed ahead. The deciduous trees had knots on their trunk that looked like huge pimples and their leaves were spotted black. The needles of the coniferous trees were orange and brown with their tops bowing down. Nipron explained that the disease had grown and spread, ravaging the trees like wildfire. It began when Ratch had taken over the palace. Snow grew heavy and whipped in circling gusts around the tiny group. Nipron stopped at a clump of dead and splintered trees near the edge of the forest.

He directed them to find large pieces of wood they could use to build a shelter. There were piles of dead wood, limbs, and large pieces of trees. So, they scurried as quick as they could to bring them to Dinky. Dinky's abilities stunned Rudy and Billy. As soon as pieces of wood were piled, Dinky worked them into a sturdy shelter to provide protection from the wind and snow. He then directed them to pack the three sides with snow to curb the sharp, strong winds that could seep into the shelter.

Once the shelter was built, Nipron directed them to quickly gather enough wood to light a bonfire and to hold the cold and darkness at bay. Everyone ate the last of their food in silence. Rudy noticed the others were also chewing their food longer than necessary. *Their throats must be like mine. Tight with fear.*

As Dinky put more wood on the fire, the howls in the woods built to a crescendo. Ten dark beings stalked out of the woods.

"Niii, Niiiii," Rudy struggled to talk but couldn't. He remembered the serf back in the cave.

"I see them," Nipron said. He ordered everyone to get behind him and for Billy and Dinky to touch Rudy. "We know the key will protect you, so don't worry." Nipron turned and walked away from them, toward the group of ten dark beings.

"Nipron, come back here! Dang! Silly old fool!" Dinky started to follow Nipron but Rudy and Billy pulled him back, tightly holding on to him.

The black serfs surrounded Nipron. Two came at him. He raised both hands as light shot forward filling them with light. They swelled until they burst into small pieces. The others rushed in, thinking he couldn't take them all at once. Nipron began twirling like a merry-go-round, out of control, with light flooding each serf until they were no more than pieces of black floating in the wind.

Four more rushed out of the forest at him. His back was to them. Rudy and Billy screamed for him to turn around. Nipron very slowly and methodically turned and raised his hands, sending blistering rays of light, filling them so that they too burst in the night.

Another four had started to approach but then stopped and backed toward the forest. Suddenly their movements froze, and they were pulled forward as if by an invisible string. Their arms were flailing to go backwards, but the invisible string pulled them quickly. Straight to Nipron.

CHAPTER 10

Nipron raised his arms once again to destroy the remaining serfs. He staggered back to the fire exhausted. Nipron sat by the smoldering flames with his head in his hands. Finally breaking the silence, he said, "Soon, we will meet Ratch. You need to know a few more things. Our world has been covered with evil. Evil so terrible it sucks the lifeblood out of the earth. You can see how even the land is dying." He poked the fire with a stick, sending sparks into the air. "When truth is made to appear evil, and evil is made to appear good, we sicken and slowly die. When truth and light are gone, there is no hope."

"Yeah, like those Dark Knights," Dinky said.

"Yes, like the Dark Knights. Once, we could count on them to protect the people from evil and from destroying the world we live in. But now, they are the ones killing and plundering the countryside."

Nipron stood up in front of the fire. The light reflecting behind him caused him to look dark and foreboding. "Truth makes us strong and drives out fear so that we have a boldness that evil can't conquer. We fight and struggle against all odds so that our children and grandchildren can live in a world of light and truth."

"The books at the guardian's keep told me the one weakness that Ratch has is 'light.' Light can destroy him!" Nipron pounded his fist into his hand and continued. "We will find him only in darkness. You saw how I was able to destroy the serfs with a ball of light? I have enough light to destroy Ratch's serf but not enough to destroy Ratch. Enough to weaken him so that we can use the key. I need all the help you can give me. Rudy, do you have anything we could use in your backpack that will give us more light?"

Rudy and Billy rummaged through the backpack. Billy grabbed the trucker's flashlight and waved it in the air. "Watch this! It lights up the whole area."

"AAggggg, I'm blind," Dinky cried.

Billy quickly turned it off.

"Sorry, Dinky. I didn't mean to aim it at you."

Staggering with his arms in front of him, Dinky wailed, "Nipron, all I see are spots in front of my eyes!"

Billy rushed to Dinky to help him. "I'm really sorry, but the spots will go away and you'll see again. It's just so dark here and your eyes are not used to the brightness."

After about five minutes, Dinky settled down and wiped his brow. "Whew, talk about light! Thank goodness I can see again. I thought you blinded me!"

Assured that Dinky could see again, Billy showed him how to use the powerful flashlight.

"Look at the forest! You can see how the trees are throwing their branches into the air crying for help," Billy said.

"This just might do it," Nipron said.

Rudy was still rummaging in the backpack, carelessly throwing things on the ground, when a roll of silver glittering ribbon unraveled close to the fire. It caught the light from the fire and shone brilliantly.

Nipron hurried over to the ribbon and stared at it. "Is it hot? Look at the shine and light it reflects."

"What? No. It's not hot. It's a roll of ribbon."

"What are you doing with all that ribbon?" asked Nipron.

Rudy was glad it was dark so Billy couldn't see how red his face was. "Billy is the one that always catches fish. Always. I mean I never really catch a fish. One time, I caught a minnow. I read somewhere that fish are attracted to shiny objects and saw this role of ribbon. . . "

"Why such a huge roll when you only need a small piece?" interrupted Billy.

"Never mind that, we can really use this. See how the light bounces back and forth on it?" Nipron observed.

Billy tore off a strip and wrapped it around his wrist. "We can wrap it around our wrists. It has tape on the back to make it stick. We can even make headbands and shields on our shirts."

"Are you serious?" Dinky asked. "What if the stuff won't ever come off?"

Rudy tore off a piece. He linked it around his wrist and then started to peel it off. "See how easy that is? We may not have enough for our bodies, but maybe for our head and arms."

Dinky took the ribbon that Rudy had crumpled and examined it. Carefully, he wrapped it around his hand. Just as carefully, he unwrapped it with a smile of discovery.

Nipron paced back and forth. "We must go deeper into the woods to get to the passageway. Ratch will be there. He knows we are here and that means he has a great source of a power that won't diminish without a great deal of light."

Stammering, Rudy asked, "He knows we're here right now? Does that mean he knows our plan?"

"He senses our presence but doesn't know exactly where we are. Otherwise, he would have sent more of his workers to greet us. I think those that I 'zapped,' as Billy would say, just happened to stumble on us." Nipron pointed at the woods. "Before we enter, we must have our plans laid out because the woods are his realms, and he controls everything that happens in there."

Rudy asked, "What happens once we are in there?"

"When you see a greenish glow, Ratch will be there. Watch for my signal to spread out in front of him."

Dinky knotted his face into a mass of wrinkles. "Let me get

this straight. You want us to stand like ducks in a row while you're holding the key?"

"Yes."

"Dang! What's to keep Ratch from burning us up first?"

Nipron patted Dinky's shoulder. "He can't. We'll be too close to him. If he tried, he would engulf himself in the fire."

"But how are we going to find Ratch if it's so dark?" Rudy asked.

"Very simple," Nipron answered. He drew a small stone out of his pocket that began to glow. Suddenly, light exploded and illuminated the sky and then slowly disappeared making the night darker. "These are night stones. They are rare and difficult to find. I have three more. They shine only for a few moments and then the light passes away. Most of the time, I will be able to see in the darkness, but there will be times that he will make it so that I won't be able to see at all."

"Could Pega take us there?" Rudy asked. "He did make us walk through the clouds."

"Yes, yes, if he were here." Nipron's voice trailed off. He did say he would meet us in the north. . . "

"Is there any way to call him here?" Rudy asked.

"No, besides the time is not right," Nipron said.

"What's time got to do with anything?" Billy asked.

Flickering flames bounced shadows off Nipron's face

revealing the determined set of his jaw. "I now understand why the Knight of Light said I have the answers. Passageways are places one enters other worlds. Just like you two did. It's like a window of time. You can enter a different world only around noon or a short time thereafter of each day because the length of the shadows are just right. But you also need a key, a special guardian key. Timing is everything, so we have to be at the passageway where Ratch is, shortly around noon."

"Dang, why don't we just go through a tunnel in the earth to get there?" asked Dinky.

"We are too close to the Demon of Chaos. The minute we went underground, the soil and air would be blacker and thicker than sorghum molasses. He would squeeze the air so tight that we'd be gasping for breath."

"Diddle squat! That's enough! We get the picture."

"How are we going to get there?" Rudy asked.

"We have to wait for Pega. He will help us get there. Until then, there is nothing we can do. So we may as well get some sleep."

The cold encased them as they huddled together to keep warm. Rudy heard foreboding sounds erupt from the pitch-black forest. He thought he heard, "You're lost, lost, forever lost." Shivering and huddling closer to Billy, he tried to sleep. Sleep became impossible as the howls swelled like a rock concert out of control. *I know I'm afraid but Nipron knows what he's doing, so I have to keep the faith.* Finally, he asked Dinky if he was asleep.

"Diddly squat! Who can sleep with all that noise?"

"Would you teach me some more Tae Kwon Do moves? I can't sleep either."

By the light of the fire, Rudy and Dinky practiced. Rudy felt he was improving until Dinky flipped him twice in a row. He did catch Dinky one time and was able to prevent being tossed on his back again. Soon they were sweating. When the sounds got louder, they would practice faster and harder. Finally exhausted, they quit and fell asleep in their bedrolls.

In the morning, Rudy was the first to wake. He stared at the black forest as it loomed into view through the swirling snow. His eyes strayed to last night's fire that had dwindled to a few red coals. Struggling to get out of the tangle of blankets, the blast of cold air took his breath away. Billy woke and helped Rudy haul more wood to the fire. A great many trees from the diseased forest had fallen and lay scattered about. The trees were so rotten, they only had to tug a little and a piece would break off.

Nipron and Dinky sat talking. Eventually, they got up and found three large poles and strapped them together. Tying a pot in the middle of the poles, they placed it over the fire to melt snow. Once the snow melted, Nipron pulled another pan out of his coat and dipped it into the water, then added a few grains of green weed. Once the water thickened, he gave everyone a cup of green water from the pan. Rudy tasted the thick green liquid and was surprised. It tasted like pea soup. Nipron told them to keep the kettle filled with water by scooping the snow into it and to make sure there was enough fire to keep it hot.

Rudy wondered how Nipron pulled a kettle and pan from his coat when it didn't look like anything was in his pockets, but he was too busy looking for more wood to burn to ask.

The sun rose high in the sky. Nipron said, "I must go into the woods a short way and I must have the key, Rudy." He placed his hands on Rudy's shoulders and looked him in the eye. "You are brave and have learned to face your fears. The key didn't make you that way. It just showed you how brave you really can be. You are the one that banished fear, not the key."

Worry and doubt wrapped around Rudy like a cocoon, imprisoning him so he could not move. Finally, Nipron's soothing voice broke through, and Rudy slowly lifted the key over his head and gave it to Nipron.

Nipron went into the woods and disappeared. Rudy could not sit by the fire and listen to the strong howls. They filled the air with painful sounds that grabbed at their ears. He jumped up, "Billy, Dinky said I was getting good at my moves to protect myself. Why don't you and I practice? I know you took classes on how to block someone's moves. It will help me when I meet Tank and Otis again."

Without warning, Billy charged Rudy. He was shocked, but then remembered how Dinky told him to control his movements and to think about what he was doing. Rudy turned in a circle away from Billy. Billy was going too fast to stop, so Rudy used that momentum and pushed him even further ahead. Turning, Billy had a surprised grin on his face and came at Rudy more slowly. Billy reached out and grabbed Rudy's' arm ready to flip him. All of a sudden,

Rudy turned into Billy and grabbed his head and flipped him over. Billy lay there a minute not believing what happened. He jumped up and they both began to move and tumble and flip and roll around on the ground. Finally, Rudy said, "I give."

Billy pulled Rudy up, "You will have no trouble handling Tank and Otis. Dinky taught you well." He laughed, "I want to be there to see their surprised faces."

The howls in the forest grew louder and more fierce, then suddenly, all was quiet and a swarm of fruit bats came out of the forest straight at them. They were screeching like a hundred rusty hinges. Rudy and Billy picked up chunks of wood and started swinging.

Dinky yelled, "Get the light, get the light!" He was soon covered by the largest of the fruit bats.

Finally, it penetrated Rudy's mind what Dinky was saying, and he ran over to the backpack and turned on the flash torch. The light was so bright that the bats screamed and flew back into the forest. All but one. The large one that had Dinky pinned down, reared back, and opened its mouth wide. Without thinking, Rudy ran over and jammed the light into its mouth. It exploded into pieces of black, flying everywhere.

"Dinky, are you okay?" Rudy's knees felt week and he sat down. "I can't believe I did that. I didn't even stop to think how scary it was seeing that bat go for your throat. I guess that is what friends do, like you do for me, Billy, when those bullies are after me."

"If it hadn't been for you, I would have been a goner, Rudy. That thing was trying to eat me. I never saw or heard of a fruit bat attacking a dwarf. Never, ever!" Dinky shouted.

Billy examined Dinky's neck closely. "Thank goodness you had the light, Rudy. Dinky didn't even get a scratch."

With a sigh of relief, Rudy said, "I think we need to collect more wood and build a bigger fire for the night."

All three hurried, gathering a huge pile of wood, and built a bonfire that roared to the sky. "We'll have to take turns in the night feeding it to make sure nothing else comes out of those woods," said Dinky.

When the fire was big enough, they all sat and stared at the fire. Dinky sat with his blanket drawn tightly around him, his head down. Billy sat next to him with his arm around Dinky.

"Are you okay, Dinky?"

Dinky looked up with eyes haunted by his fears. "Yes, but I'm worried Nipron may not come back."

It was quiet for a long time.

"Dinky, he'll come back, don't worry. He has to. We don't have any magic to fight Ratch. The Knight promised that he would have the answers." Rudy patted his arm. "Dang! It's only an idiot that isn't afraid when there's reason to be."

A bleak smile briefly crossed Dinky's face and then vanished.

They all sat and stared as the snow swirled around them.

Briefly, the dead forest would come into view and then vanish as the snow blew harder. At the same time, the howls became louder and seemed to be calling out, "You're lost, lost. . ."

Evening came and went without anyone thinking of supper.

Through the gusting snow, they saw a huge white cloud carrying something on its back. Nipron!

"Sagacious," Billy cried, as he ran toward the dragon. "What happened to Nipron?"

"Agh, it's one of the demon workers," Dinky cried. The shadows from the light from the fire seem to be playing tricks with their eyes but suddenly caught a gleam of something shiny.

"It's Nipron! Look at the key!" Rudy yelled. He started to run toward Nipron, but Dinky pulled him back.

He struggled to get away. Rudy yelled. "It's not a demon of chaos! Come on. Billy is already helping Nipron. Can't you see the key?"

Dinky looked hard at the bedraggled form. He finally saw the key and ran past Rudy and pushed Billy aside.

Sagacious knelt and let Nipron slide into their arms. His face was twisted in pain. His swollen purple eyes fluttered below the deep gashes that lined his forehead. His arms and legs were red and blackened from burns and he smelled like a burnt charred piece of firewood. Dinky laid him gently on a blanket and removed Nipron's leather coat that hung in shreds.

Sagacious said, "Take care of him and make him well so that when Pega comes, he will be able to deal with Ratch." He looked at Rudy and then Billy and said, "You need to be brave." And with that, he flew up and melted in the sky.

"I sure wish he would stick around so we could get some answers," Billy said. "What does he mean? He always flies away before I can finish asking my questions."

CHAPTER 11

Rudy, Billy, and Dinky walked slowly toward their campfire, gently carrying Nipron. With each step, they heard him whimper with pain. Rudy sat down cradling Nirpon and Billy sat next to him patting Nipron's arm. Dinky fumbled to get a mixture of herbs from his pocket. "Dang! I need a cup of water," he mumbled.

Rudy eased Nipron over to Billy and ran to the tripod and brought water. He thought it was a good thing that Nipron built this tripod and had them heat water. Dinky grabbed the cup and mixed the herbs in the hot liquid. "Is that soup?" Billy asked.

Shaking his head, Dinky replied, "No, it's a potion. Nipron told me how to use it if he got back."

Slowly, Nipron drank while Dinky gently wiped his face and arms. Nipron's hand had a deep gash which Dinky cleaned and wrapped. He then covered him in blankets and rocked Nipron while quietly weeping.

"Why did Nipron go into the forest, Dinky?" asked Rudy.

Dinky answered, "He wanted to try to get Ratch by himself. He didn't want to put any of us in danger. He was afraid that if he didn't try, Ratch would come out of the forest and hurt us. Dang! Silly old fool. He wanted us to have enough light to protect ourselves in case he didn't make it back."

Cradling the flashlight, Rudy said, "That's why he didn't take the flash torch. Is he going to be all right?"

Dinky didn't answer, he just kept rocking Nipron.

The rest of the night, the howls grew more savage, sending chills into the small group around the fire. They took turns feeding the fire and holding Nipron. He needed to stay warm— not only from the blankets but from their body heat as well.

By daybreak, the wind and snow stopped. Shadowed by clouds hiding the warmth of the sun, the small group huddled around Nipron.

"Dinky, how did Nipron get so badly bruised and hurt. Why didn't the key protect him like it did us?" Rudy asked.

Dinky shook his head, "Nipron knew you would ask that. He said to tell you that it would protect mortals, but not questors. The questors are to use the key to help others and to open windows of time to other worlds. He wanted to try it on his own, to own a window of time to send Ratch back. Silly old fool."

The morning cold was brittle, the trees dropping limbs with loud cracks breaking the silence. Billy and Rudy gathered wood to keep the fire going. Dinky mixed another potion for

Nipron, who drank it slowly. But he remained as quiet as death. Shortly before noon, a sound like a hundred beating wings headed straight for them. Pega had arrived.

He immediately went to Nipron, lowered his head and nuzzled him. Pega reared high into the air for he could feel the darkness that was poisoning Nipron. "Unwrap him from those blankets and look at his hand."

Quickly, Dinky unwrapped Nipron and saw that his hand was blackish-purple and swollen three times its normal size. The long, jagged cut festered and oozed pus. "Bring boiling water from the fire," Pega commanded.

Running quickly to the fire that had a kettle hanging from a tripod, Rudy dipped a pan into the hot water and ran to Pega.

Pega ordered Rudy, "Hold the pan steady. Dinky, take your knife to make a small incision in the wound."

Shaking, Dinky made a small cut. The skin split open like a zipper, thick black pus pouring out.

"Quickly, slide Nipron's hand into the pan. Now!"

The water sizzled and created a horrible stench in the air. When the sizzling stopped, Pega ordered Rudy to take Nipron's hand out of the water and to throw the pan and blackened water into the fire. The fire ballooned with black angry smoke in the air with laughter that sounded like a knife scraping on a bottle.

Pega said, "In a few minutes, he should wake up. He'll be weak and hungry. Dinky, get some food ready."

"Dang! We ran out yesterday."

"I think not! Look in that boy's long bag," Pega ordered.

Dinky didn't want to leave Nipron but decided looking would be better than having Pega stomp the stuffing out of him. He muttered under his breath, "Diddly squat! There's no food in Rudy's backpack."

"Hey, where did this ham come from?" Dinky cried.

Pega answered, "Ratch isn't the only one that has magic."

Nipron opened his eyes and looked at Pega, "Ah, dear friend, I failed."

"Not yet. Remember you were supposed to wait for me. But then you always were stubborn and had difficulty waiting. Rest now and have some food. You will need your strength."

Rudy, Billy, and Dinky ran over to the backpack. They couldn't believe the food Dinky was pulling out. Not only bread and cheese but cakes too!

Laughing, Billy carried food over to Nipron while taking bites of his small cake. "I know you didn't pack this food, but it sure is delicious."

Dinky hurried to Nipron, trying to get him to eat. He struggled to sit up. "One thing at a time, please. I can't eat everything all at once."

After they had eaten, Rudy asked, "What happened in the forest?"

In a weak voice Nipron said, "I'm not really sure. Ratch said I would forget. I almost had him! That much I do remember. But then he grabbed my hand." After a sip of water, he continued. "It was a struggle, and his evil almost consumed me." Tears welling in his eyes, and in a strangled voice he continued, "Like the knights, I almost believed that evil was good. It would have been so easy to believe what he said. Then, out of the corner of my eye, I saw the Knight of Light standing close by, reminding me of truth and light."

"You don't remember because Ratch is afraid. I can see the spell he put on you to make you forget, but I can't break it," Pega said.

Nipron smiled, "For some reason, I have a plan. Maybe the Knight of Light was there and helped me formulate a plan before I fell unconscious. Only, my plan is very dangerous. Rudy, I still need to wear this key at all times because Ratch will go after me first. He feels that if he gets me, then all of you will be easily taken care of and he won't have to worry about being sent back to the Demon of Chaos. What he doesn't know is that Pega is here and will see you all safely out before he can do anything."

"I'm ready," Billy said. "I think I am, anyway,"

Clearing his throat, Rudy also agreed and wondered if he looked as afraid as Billy. Nipron told them about his plan, and everyone went to work. They took the spool of silver ribbon and wrapped it around their arms and then made headbands. The rest of the ribbon they used to wrap Pega's hooves.

The sun was directly above them, so they knew it was noon. "Let's go," ordered Pega. Everyone followed. Pega told them to hang on to one another and not let go. The path was narrow and if they strayed, the black serfs were certain to grab them and haul them into the depths of darkness.

Nipron led. Pega followed with Rudy, Billy, and Dinky bringing up the rear. One minute they were by the fire, the next they were slowly walking in coal-black darkness on the murky ground. Following Pega, and holding on to his tail, Rudy screamed, "I can't take the next step. I don't feel solid ground. There is nothing to step on!"

Nipron floated to where Rudy stood and used a moon stone. The area lit up and where Rudy was to step was a large gap. The ground had fallen away. Evil had eaten the earth and the soil just disappeared.

Nipron said, "Everyone, back up. Pega, I have to ask you to let our three conquerors ride on your back. I know under normal circumstances you would never allow it. But we are desperate because Ratch is eating the ground away underneath them as they walk. He is determined to attack us!"

Pega had never allowed anyone to sit on his back, but he willingly knelt beside Rudy and the others.

His voice more urgent, Nipron said, "Move quickly and climb on his back." The three didn't have to be told twice. They scrambled up, quietly shivering with fear. Pega stood and they continued on their way, the ground falling away. Dark forms jutted in and out trying to reach them, but Pega's magic protected them.

All at once, everything was darker and blacker than before. They could see nothing, not even a shadow or the hand in front of their face. All the sound seemed to have been sucked away and they couldn't even hear their own breathing. It was so dark and black that Rudy couldn't help but think that this is what it would look like if you were in a barrel of black oil.

Nipron took a moon stone out, and the light shined brightly in the darkness. They could see Ratch who was surrounded by an orange glow that intensified as the moonstone brightened. It quivered with each breath Ratch took. His massive form towered over them. His huge and twisted muscles flexed. Ratch had gigantic hands shaped like hammers with long sharp quill-like fingernails. Evil pulsated through his pores and anger pulsated like a black beacon. His face twisted as he spat out, "So you didn't learn the first time, Nipron."

Everyone was frozen with fear. No one could move. Nipron came out of his haze of fear and lifted the key. A bright light began to shine from the key. The key's light awakened everyone from their fear and they climbed off Pega. Slowly, they spread out in a half circle. The light from the key shot straight at Ratch and hit him in the chest.

The key grew brighter and brighter. Rudy looked around and saw the Knight of Light sitting on his horse behind Nipron. He was feeding Nipron's light.

Guess we didn't need my puny flashlight, Rudy thought.

Light bounced off the silver ribbon that adorned arms, heads, and Pegas's hooves. No matter how much he struggled, the light held Ratch in its grip. The light was so bright it brought tears to all their eyes. The light had a power and life of its own. It surrounded Ratch, shrinking him smaller and smaller.

Rudy saw Nipron take the key from his neck and hold it out in front of him. Suddenly, a bolt of light erupted from the key. It hit Ratch in the chest, pulling him toward Nipron, who was slowly walking backward. As Nipron walked, dark beings tried to attack him, but the Knight of Light kept shooting rays of light destroying the dark beings. They exploded in pieces that sprayed in all directions. Finally, Nipron stood between two enormous black rocks that jutted skyward into a point. As soon as Ratch stood in front of him, Nipron stepped to the side and laid the key next to a huge boulder. A black hole opened with a wind that sucked everything nearby into it. Everything but Nipron who stood calmly watching.

Rudy couldn't believe that Nipron was in the eye of the storm and the wind didn't seem to touch him. His eyes were peaceful and calm as blackness and wind raged around him. Rudy, Billy, and Dinky crowded closer to Pega as the wind whipped the ribbon from their arms and heads. They felt themselves being pulled toward the hole. The only thing that saved them from following Ratch into that black hole was clinging to Pega's mane and tail.

Ratch struggled against the pull to no avail and was sucked into the void as he screamed, "You haven't seen the last of me, Nipron!" The black hole vanished.

Nipron picked up the key and walked toward his shaken partners. The darkness had disappeared with the wind and light filled the forest where they stood. The fragrance of spring filled the air. Trees were no longer dead and diseased but were budding and leafing in a split second. Like a spreading flood, dirt changed into thick carpet grass beneath their feet and flowers bloomed in abundance. Birds and forest animals appeared, causing the forest to become alive with their musical sounds.

In awe, Rudy said, "This is a beautiful place. Ratch and his evil just hid it."

People who had been imprisoned by Ratch were freed and streamed out of the woods. Worn and ragged, they cheered and sang as Nipron and Pega bowed to them.

"I need to bring the healers here for the people," Pega said. "Your father would be proud of you, Nipron."

"We couldn't have done it without you, my dear friend. We have much work to do."

Pega was already in the air. "I'll bring the healers back quickly, then we can catch up on old times."

"Did you see the Knight of Light helping you, Nipron?" Billy asked.

"I most certainly did! I'm learning that he is always with me and that only in the most needful times will he appear."

Rudy laughed. "It seems as though he wanted you to believe in yourself and think things through. Just like you and Dinky told me to do."

"You are so right, Rudy. . . " "Nipron's eyes watered, and his voice croaked.

Rudy felt a sudden wave of homesickness. "Guess it's time for us to head home."

Nipron led them to a place in the forest where the tree branches made an arch.

"Hey, this looks exactly like the place where I met the Knight of Light," Rudy exclaimed.

"This is a passageway called Kneelgrove, and it is the way back to your world," Nipron said. He laid the key next to a large tree. An opening appeared, mirroring another forest like the one they were leaving.

Billy ran through the Window of Time, waving his goodbye and yelling, "Here's my fishing pole!"

"Remember, Rudy. You are brave. You don't have to be afraid of everyday things," Dinky said.

"I won't. I promise. Bye!" Rudy stepped through the doorway, into the forest surrounding his home. Billy greeted him with a big bear hug and asked, "Do you think anyone is going to believe us?"

Shaking his head and turning for home Rudy said, "Not in a million years."

"Hey, where are you going? Aren't we going fishing?" Billy asked.

"Not me! I have to climb my tree house and walk across the bridge," Rudy called over his shoulder. Billy went in the opposite direction to fish. Rudy's excitement grew with each step he took, until. . .

Tank and Otis crashed out of the trees, landing on the road, just by Rudy's feet.

"Well, well. Your bodyguard isn't with you, now is he?" said Tank.

Otis slapped his fist into his hand, "We got you now!"

"Oh yeah? Come and get me!" yelled Rudy.

For a long second, Tank and Otis were too stunned to move. Where was the Rudy who always ran away screaming? Still not deterred, Tank got into Rudy's face and yelled, "You better be afraid!

While Tank yelled, Otis snuck around and jumped on Rudy's back, his arms around Rudy's neck. Rudy turned and flipped Otis on his back. Otis lay on the hard dirt, struggling to get his breath. Tank charged Rudy, running straight at him. Rudy stepped aside, tripping and pushing Tank hard, sending him sprawling on the gravel road. Tank sat up, spitting out gravel. His arms and hands bled with gravel rash.

"I'm not afraid of you two anymore, so leave me alone!" Rudy turned and headed home, feeling good about the moves that Dinky had taught him.

I think I'll sign up for some more Tae Kwon Do.

Rudy

Billy

Nipron

Dinky

A furlet

Sagacious

The Knight of Light

About the Author
Sharon Leino

The oldest girl in a family of 11, Sharon always had a great imagination. As a child, she expressed herself through poetry, pouring out her feelings about love, adventure, anger, and being bullied. When her father died, she quit writing and threw away all her poetry. She's asked herself why, but just decided that, "Sometimes we do some dumb things in our lives."

As a grownup, Sharon's career as an educator and special education curriculum developer found her writing reports and grants. She kept extensive journals of her travels with her beloved husband to the many countries and states they visited.

Her childhood love of writing resurfaced with a vengeance when she retired and became a Texas snowbird. After joining various writer's groups, it became clear she had a passion for writing inspiring books for children. Just as this happened, her husband lost his sight, and her stories were packed away to make room for their new adventure that was full of trials but also love and joy. Florida became their home where Sharon still lives, making a new life for herself on her own. Her days are full of volunteering at church, creating jewelry as an amateur silversmith, and of course, writing.

www.sharonleinoauthor.com

Made in the USA
Columbia, SC
29 August 2022